T0188649

SIMPLE CREATURES

ROBERT McGILL

COACH HOUSE BOOKS, TORONTO

first edition

Published with the generous assistance of the Canada Council for the Arts and the Ontario Arts Council. Coach House Books also acknowledges the support of the Government of Canada through the Canada Book Fund and the Government of Ontario through the Ontario Book Publishing Tax Credit.

LIBRARY AND ARCHIVES CANADA CATALOGUING IN PUBLICATION

Title: Simple creatures / Robert McGill.
Names: McGill, Robert, 1976- author
Description: First edition.
Identifiers: Canadiana (print) 20240443322 | Canadiana (ebook) 20240445783 | ISBN 9781552454930 (softcover) | ISBN 9781770568198 (EPUB) | ISBN 9781770568204 (PDF)
Subjects: LCGFT: Short stories.
Classification: LCC PS8625.G54 S56 2024 |DDC C813/.6—dc23

Simple Creatures is available as an ebook: ISBN 978 1 77056 819 8 (EPUB), ISBN 978 1 77056 820 4 (PDF)

Purchase of the print version of this book entitles you to a free digital copy. To claim your ebook of this title, please email sales@chbooks.com with proof of purchase. (Coach House Books reserves the right to terminate the free digital download offer at any time.)

For Siobhan

CONTENTS

NOBODY GOES TO VANCOUVER TO DIE

Everyone is born with the same amount of energy but uses it up at different speeds. That's how it seems to Gloria sometimes. She spent more than two decades chasing four kids around the farmhouse, then ran out of steam. Morley spent most of those years in the apple orchard, standing on ladders, never moving any faster than he felt like moving. Now, watch him go. She sits in her chair, cheering, as he makes the other guys look like chumps, like they should be in a home.

'You made them look like chumps!' she shouts with a laugh. Second place still hasn't crossed the finish line.

Morley jogs across the track to the place in the stands where he put her before the race.

'Don't shout like that,' he growls. 'You're embarrassing yourself.'

After that, he struts down lane eight in his body suit, looking like Hercules in a geriatric ward. The others are just geezers in underwear. A bunch of old bags farther down the stands are waving and whistling, and he waves back as if Gloria isn't right there. That's okay, though. They're just old bags.

At the far end of the straightaway, the little group of protesters stands waiting: half a dozen women in matching tracksuits, all grey-haired and grinning like hyenas. As Morley draws near, a chant goes up from them – 'EQUAL RIGHTS, OPEN RACES!' – and they hoist their hand-painted placards with glee: 'YWCA Witches 4 Attie Fairwater.' 'Only Racing Her Will Lift Our Curse!'

'*Fast AF vs. Scared AF.*' '*Race Her! You're MORLEY Obligated!*' Morley doesn't turn their way, as if he's the only person who hasn't noticed them, but Gloria can tell he's heard. If she were closer, she'd see that little vein on his neck throbbing, the one that pops out only when he's supremely pissed off.

Attie Fairwater stands among the protesters, laughing along with them, her long silver hair hanging over her placard. In one moment, it looks like a medallist's ribbon; in another, like iron bars she's rattling.

'Come on, Morley,' Attie shouts. 'Be a man and look me in the eye.'

That's enough to get his goat up.

'Go back to the hotel and rest,' he says. 'Save that wind for your race tomorrow.'

'Why don't you just admit you're chickenshit?' she replies.

'What did you say?' From the look on his face, Gloria knows he isn't expressing disbelief; he just didn't hear her properly.

'Chickenshit,' Attie says. 'That's what you are.'

This time, it's clear that Morley hears her.

He's used to having everyone's eyes on him, but not their ears; he splutters a bit and doesn't say anything. Then, in a seeming fit of inspiration, he raises his hands to his armpits and waves his elbows up and down, bobbing his head at the same time. With his spiked feet, he paws at the track so convincingly that Gloria thinks he could bring up worms. The idiot. She has seen this act before, on the farm, in private. It was funny then. It wouldn't have been if she'd known it would make an appearance here. He goes like that halfway up the track, seemingly unaware of the looks people are giving him, as if he really has turned into a rooster heading for the henhouse. He's the world champion for his age, and he's ridiculous.

Gloria feels she should be happy right now. She has worried about Morley and Attie Fairwater: all of those meets together, and the two of them so often mentioned in the same articles.

But she's only relieved that no one's broadcasting the race. That's pretty funny, seeing how she used to think these meets should have a television deal.

'Nobody wants to watch old people running,' Morley replied when she told him. 'They want the real guns, the young muscles.'

The real guns, she thought. Sometimes he even talked like a kid.

'Well, I don't want those things,' she said. 'Young muscles are boring. Anyone can be young and muscular. If you're old and muscular, that's something. People think being old means being weak and useless. Let's put you on TV and watch them eat their words.'

He's right, though. If he goes out in a tank top, people aren't impressed; they look at him like he's a freak. Maybe they're right, too. He just bought a leather jacket. He has a tattoo of his world record on his bicep. She has seen other competitors, even some of the ones in their eighties and nineties, with the same thing. The world championships are one big freak show. The organizers have asked Morley to give a speech at the banquet, because, of all the freaks, he's the freakiest.

'Twelve-year-old boys,' he said once. 'At all-comers meets, twelve-year-olds beat me, Gloria. Nobody wants to see an old man run.'

Morley can race the 800 metres in two minutes and twenty-nine seconds. He's seventy-six, and that is a world record. When he gets depressed, she reminds him of that, as though it weren't already there on his arm.

'A world record,' she tells him. 'You're pretty special.'

Normally, he goes to meets by himself, and Julie comes up from the city to stay with Gloria. It's a long drive, but Julie's still single, without any kids, and says she doesn't mind.

'I'm sorry, sweetie,' Gloria said to her the last time. 'You're forty-five, you shouldn't have to babysit.'

'I'm not babysitting you, Mom,' Julie said, rubbing Gloria's neck. 'You're too ugly to be a baby.'

Gloria laughed. 'I'm about as wrinkly now as you were the day you were born.'

Julie smiles, and Gloria knows it's not because the line's funny; Julie just likes it when Gloria talks about the past. It proves she can remember. You turn seventy, and suddenly your kids are on non-stop Alzheimer's alert.

'Who are you? What are you doing in my house?' Gloria said one time when Julie came in.

'Mom, it's me, it's Julie,' she whispered. Then she realized. 'Oh, you're such an asshole.'

Gloria has come to Vancouver with Morley because it's the world championships and because she wants to keep an eye on him. At the stadium, it's mostly old people milling around: the athletes and their supporters. There are no fans, really, just supporters: husbands and wives, children, grandchildren. Some of the competitors are still in their thirties and look like they could qualify for the real world championships instead of slumming it in the age-group version. Then there are the athletes who are Morley's age. Gloria wonders why some of them bother. On the first day, he wins the 400-metre heats and the 1500-metre final. At his age, there are no heats for the 1500-metre race; they just line up everybody on the track, and anyone who finishes gets a standing ovation from the spectators who can stand. The St. John Ambulance people always look nervous before the 1500-metre race, but nobody's croaked yet, at least not at any meet that Gloria has attended. At this age, people are savvy. They know what they're capable of. They aren't going to travel all the way to Vancouver to die on a running track. Still, some of them are pretty pathetic, with their spindly calves, their sagging guts, and their sad, shuffling gaits. Morley nearly laps a few of them.

'Why don't you enter all the events?' she asked him yesterday when she saw the starting lists with the seed times. 'The 100, the 200 – hell, why not the long jump? You'd clean up.'

He looked at her like she was from another planet, and he explained that he needed to focus on just a few races if he wanted more world records.

At sixty-five, he gave up ice cream and pizza, and his belly melted away. She was happy for him, of course she was. For her part, she'd been on countless diets, deprived herself of every food you could imagine, and her weight had kept creeping up. He started to train and got muscles while she got diabetes. Now, you'd never guess she's younger than he is. She sits at home in a wheelchair while he travels the world, refusing to use a cellphone or pay for long-distance charges, so that she doesn't hear from him until he's back. Then he doesn't want to talk about the trips, won't say how his races went unless she asks. Even then, all he gives her are the times, which meant nothing to her at first. When she asked him if he had a list of the world records for his events, he asked why she was interested, but eventually she found them on the internet, and now she knows his times and everyone else's better than he does.

Attie Fairwater is seventy-five and the Canadian champion for the 5000 metres.

'Attie? She's not in my league,' Morley told Gloria one time.

'Never mind your league,' she replied. 'What about mine?'

'She has a husband,' he protested.

'Wrong answer, buster.'

After the day's races, Gloria and Morley take a taxi back to the hotel and he goes down to the bar. He used to ask her if she wanted to come along, but not anymore. She's pretty sure that he and Attie have enjoyed some good heart-to-hearts, sitting in hotel bars together, before Attie started making a fuss about racing him.

Once it's an hour past the time he said he'd be back, Gloria calls reception and asks to be put through to the bar. The man who answers says Morley isn't there.

'Are you sure?' she asks. 'He's got glasses and short white hair.'

'Lady, we've got twenty guys like that tonight. There's some kind of old-timers convention in town.'

'This guy stands out. He's muscular, and he doesn't look old.'

'First you say he's old, then you say – '

'I didn't say he was old, I said white hair and glasses.'

'Hold on – ' There's a pause. 'Maybe I see him. Black leather jacket?'

'That's him. Could you tell him to come upstairs? His wife needs him.'

'Sure thing.'

When she calls again ten minutes later, she gets a different man. 'I called a little while ago about my husband,' she says. 'He hasn't returned to our room. Is he still there?'

'What's he look like?'

'Black leather jacket,' she says. 'Glasses. Short white hair.'

'No, there's nobody like that.'

She hangs up, thinking that Morley could have bribed them to lie.

'If you want to set more world records, should you be tying one on?' she said before he left.

'A couple of drinks never killed anybody,' he replied. 'A man has to live.'

She decides to go downstairs. It would be wise to call for a porter, but she isn't feeling wise. She refuses to wait here, aging without him.

Before Morley left, he helped her to change into her nightgown. Getting her clothes back on now would be too much, but she can manage her raincoat, at least. When she rolls over to the closet to tug at the coat's corner, it won't come off the hanger, and she ends up banging her leg against the wall before she finally gets the coat down and wriggles into it. The door's next. Turn and pull the knob, back up with one hand, wedge open the door with a footrest. But she can't steer straight with just one hand, and she starts to spin. Morley would already be out of the hotel by now. A young couple in the hallway pass and stare.

'Mind your own business,' says Gloria.

Once she's through the door, it's clear sailing. Normally, she and Morley would stay in a wheelchair-friendly room, but those ones were all booked because of the meet.

'Can't you ask for special treatment?' she said. 'You're the star of the show.'

'Things don't work like that,' he said.

She didn't like it. The best in the world, and no TV coverage, no hotel privileges. The only thing that running fast gets him is around the track more quickly, right back to where he started. Yet every day, he trains for hours. He watches his diet like a supermodel. He takes ice baths and vitamin supplements, does plyometrics, sees a physiotherapist weekly. The one time she asked him to explain the appeal of working so hard, he said that he likes running's simplicity. To her, it doesn't seem simple at all.

In the bar, everyone stares at her. She stops to tug her nightgown further over her legs. It's standing room only, but she doesn't say excuse me, just charges forward and makes a few shins pay, including hers.

The men on the phone were right: he's not here. At least, not now.

'Something to drink, ma'am?' asks a girl in an apron.

She shakes her head. Then, as the girl turns away, Gloria grabs at her. 'On second thought, I'll have a bourbon.'

When the girl brings it, Gloria points to the man behind the bar. 'I'd like to talk to him. Should I wheel myself there?' She says it with more bitterness than she intends, but the girl has had a long night of smiling at old people and isn't about to stop now.

'Of course not. I'll send him over.'

Gloria has almost finished her drink when the man appears. 'You're the one who called looking for the old guy, right?' he says. 'Turns out I had the wrong one. Sorry. Is there something else – ?'

'Another bourbon,' she says.

When she orders number three, the waitress shows concern. 'Will anyone be joining you? Is there somebody we should call?'

Gloria sends her off with a scowl and watches as the girl has a word with the bartender. The old lady in the wheelchair won't leave. This must be a real pickle for them. Gloria's waiting to see what will happen next when someone nearby speaks.

'You're Morley Day's wife, aren't you?'

It's Attie Fairwater, standing just a foot away.

'That's me,' says Gloria. 'And you're Attie Fairwater, the shit disturber.'

Attie's wearing slacks and a short-sleeved blouse that shows off her sinewy arms, proof that she hasn't yet fully emigrated to the land of the elderly. She just holds a passport that lets her visit when convenient.

'I don't want to cause trouble,' Attie says. 'I only want to race him.'

'He'll never race you. He says it's beneath him.'

Attie bristles but doesn't bite. 'Yes, well, listen – I'm sorry, I've forgotten your name – '

'Gloria.'

'Gloria, I only came over to see if you wanted company.'

It's Gloria's turn to bristle. 'I'm fine. Morley should be here soon.'

Attie frowns. 'Really?'

'Oh, yes,' she says. Attie's tone has her worried, though.

'I'm sure you're right,' Attie says. 'But I should tell you, he was here a little while ago, and I saw him head out with a few of the sprinters to another bar.'

Gloria sinks in her chair. 'I see.' She begins to think of excuses she could make, for herself and for him, but she's too tired. 'You don't know which bar, do you?'

'It's a few blocks up,' says Attie. 'I could take you there if you want.'

Gloria thinks about what she wants. If she goes after him, he'll have a fit, especially if she shows up in her nightgown with Attie Fairwater. He'll accuse her of conspiring against him.

Suddenly, though, she doesn't care. In fact, the idea has a certain appeal.

She asks Attie to wheel her over to the bartender, whom she pays for the drinks. Then she asks Attie to take her to the other bar.

It's the middle of August, and the air outside the hotel is still warm, though the sun was long ago swallowed by Stanley Park, its cathedral of ancient forest a barricade between downtown and the Pacific. A salty breeze off the ocean sends Attie's hair rippling behind her. How does she run with all that weight hanging off her, Gloria almost asks, but it's a stupid question. Here they are, two human beings of the same age and nationality, and Attie might as well be an alien from outer space.

'You don't mind me pushing you?' Attie asks.

'It's all right,' says Gloria. 'Morley does it all the time. I get so tired nowadays, I have no pride in it.'

'I'm sure you have other things to be proud of,' says Attie.

'Like Morley,' says Gloria, thinking that's what she means.

'Sure,' Attie says.

'There's the kids, too,' says Gloria. 'And the grandkids. Not that I can do much with them. It's terrible when the body goes. You're lucky.'

'Oh, I know it,' says Attie.

'Good on you, making the most of things.'

They're heading up the hill now, the glow of neon signs beckoning from the top.

'If I get too heavy, tell me,' says Gloria. 'We can head back.'

Attie laughs. 'I think I'll be all right.'

Gloria feels stupid for suggesting it. Attie's a champion athlete. Why would she need to rest?

'Here,' says Attie, 'let's make this interesting.'

All at once, Gloria's chair lurches forward as Attie breaks into a run, still pushing her.

'Don't you have a race tomorrow?' Gloria says over the chair's rattle.

Attie takes that as her cue to run faster. The grade proves a challenge, but once the hill crests, they really start to move, and soon they're both laughing.

'All right, enough!' cries Gloria, breathing harder than Attie, it seems.

'Can't wait to go back down,' says Attie as she brings her to a stop. Then her voice drops to a murmur. 'Gloria, I think we're here.'

She points to the marquee on the other side of the street. The Apollo. There's something strange about it. Gloria's gaze slides down to the signs around the door. 'GIRLS.' 'XXX.' '30 LIVE PERFORMANCES NIGHTLY.' An empty plastic bag scuttles across the sidewalk.

'This is where they said they were going?' Gloria asks.

Attie nods, and Gloria feels her face fill with blood.

'You did this to humiliate me,' she says.

'Gloria, honey, I didn't, really. I had no idea what kind of place it was.'

'He's not in there. He wouldn't.'

'You're right. They probably went someplace else. Let me take you back, okay?'

Gloria almost agrees. Then she imagines sitting in her chair in the hotel room. Morley returning, falling asleep in seconds, waking up and leaving for the track. The two of them flying home with nothing said.

She puts her hand on the chair's brake. 'No, I'll wait for him. You can go back if you want.'

She watches a lone man slink into the Apollo, staring at her as he goes. She imagines how she and Attie must look to him.

An old crone in a wheelchair, and a woman who could be Medusa with that mane of hair.

'Are you sure?' says Attie. 'If you'd like to talk with him, you might be better off – '

'It's none of your business.'

Attie shifts her weight from foot to foot like she's settling into starting blocks. 'Gloria, look, I guess you know this – or maybe you don't – but Morley has a bit of a reputation.'

A panic surges in her. 'Oh, I know,' she says quickly. 'He drinks too much. I don't know why he started again. He's the world champion. You'd think he'd be happier now.'

'I'm sorry,' Attie says. She gazes up at the night sky. 'Actually, it isn't the drinking – '

'No,' says Gloria. 'I know it isn't.' She's uncertain whether to demand that Attie stop speaking or to encourage her on.

'With you never joining him at meets and whatnot, everyone figured – '

'What did they figure?' Gloria snaps. She knows that 'whatnot' means her chair.

'They figured you two had … an agreement.'

Gloria's stomach churns. She shouldn't have drunk the bourbon.

'I mean, Morley's been telling people you have one,' Attie says.

Gloria thinks she's going to be sick. She hangs her head over the side of the chair, wondering which people, exactly, Morley has told. Finally, the nausea ebbs, and she sits up straight.

'Well, we do have an agreement,' she says.

'Oh,' says Attie. 'I guess it's all right, then.'

When Gloria thinks about it, she supposes it's true, in a way. There has been an agreement, just not the kind Attie's talking about. Nothing so easy or frank. More like don't ask, don't tell. Ask obliquely, don't answer. Answer obliquely, don't listen to the answer. He was out late last night, too. In the morning, he went down to get her breakfast, and when he returned, she was sitting there crying. He looked annoyed, then set her tray on the dresser and started getting ready for the meet.

'Julie called,' she told him. 'Ralph Buchan died.'

Ralph and Morley used to play golf together, before Morley realized that golf wasn't his speed. Ralph had been fighting cancer for a year.

'Jesus,' said Morley.

He sat on the nearest bed, staring at the little fridge in the corner. She thought that this was how it must have been in the age of the dinosaurs, after the asteroid hit. Some of them with rotting teeth and bloated hearts, heaving on the ground from all the long years, and some of them still darting around as though the sky wasn't clouded over with their blood about to freeze. She doubts that any of them comforted the sick. They were all dying. If you could act like it wasn't going to happen, so much the better for you.

'You should go back to the hotel now,' she says to Attie. 'You've got what you wanted out of me.'

Attie's face takes on a pained expression. 'That's not why I'm here. I've been worried about you. We don't know each other, but …'

'Let me guess. You feel sorry for me.'

Attie doesn't deny it. Well, Gloria feels sorry for herself often enough.

'You can tell me something else, then,' says Gloria. 'About him and you.'

Attie meets her gaze for just a second. 'Nothing's happened. Honestly.'

'Maybe not lately,' says Gloria. 'But before.'

Attie's forehead bunches. Then she sighs and relaxes her shoulders. 'We had dinner. A long time ago, in Helsinki. Our first meet together.'

Gloria remembers that meet. He just missed the national record. Once he got home, he barely spoke for days. He never mentioned Attie. It was only later that he started talking about the woman whose best time over five kilometres was a couple of seconds behind his.

'How did the dinner happen?' Gloria demands.

'He invited me,' Attie says. 'He didn't try anything, though. He told me at the start he wouldn't.'

'He told you?' Gloria can't imagine how he'd tell somebody that. It isn't something she wants to think about.

Attie gains an embarrassed look. 'He made a joke about me being too old for him.'

A group of seven or eight men spills out of the Apollo's door. Their faces are familiar from the track. Sure enough, Attie calls out to one by name. She pushes Gloria across the street to the Apollo, then leaves her parked on the sidewalk while she goes to speak with him. Gloria admires the smooth motion of Attie's slender frame, her spring-loaded legs.

Something isn't right, though. As Attie talks with the man, she reaches up to her chest with one hand, slowly and with seeming nonchalance, as though not to attract attention to what she's doing. Gloria sees that her breasts are lopsided. One of them looks as full and firm as a teenager's, but the other is sagging, squashed toward her armpit. Attie gives her bra strap a tug, and the breast moves back into symmetry.

'He should be out soon,' the man is saying. 'Told us he wanted to watch one more act.'

Then he does a double-take on Gloria.

'Don't worry about it,' Attie tells him. 'Go home, boys,' she says more loudly to the group, and the men head down the hill, shooting looks over their shoulders as they go.

Gloria wonders how long an act is. Three minutes? Five? Just enough time for her to give him something to think about.

She begins unzipping her raincoat.

'Are you hot, sweetie?' Attie asks, and she helps her out of the sleeves.

After that, Gloria begins to pull up her nightgown.

'What the hell are you doing?' Attie cries. She looks ready to reach out and stop her but remains in place.

'Don't worry, I'm old,' says Gloria, yanking to get the rest of the nightgown out from under her. 'Old people have no shame. They go senile, they're always doing crazy things.' She has it up around her waist now. 'He likes strip shows, doesn't he?'

'Oh, honey,' says Attie. 'Don't do this.'

But now the nightgown's up around Gloria's neck. As she slides it off her arms, the air prickles her skin. The sensation makes her remember the last time she was naked out of doors, forty years ago, swimming at night in the grotto at the provincial park. She and Morley had gone with the Sterlings, the four of them leaving all their kids with the girl down the road. It was September, and Georgian Bay was losing its summer warmth. Gloria's dare got them all to do it. She could feel the husband, she's forgotten his name, watching her as she undressed, while Irene was already in the water, right in front of Morley, who was too busy with his belt buckle to notice. Gloria dove deeper than any of them, staying down there so long that Morley started worrying. When she finally surfaced, he splashed over to embrace her and nearly drowned them both.

Now, it's Attie who moves toward her. Gloria waves her off.

'Okay, fine,' says Attie. 'But if the cops show, I don't know you.' She crosses her eyes and grins.

Morley isn't the next person out. There are several others, two or three at a time. They glance at Gloria with puzzlement or leering smiles, as if to say they're in on whatever joke she's playing. She's prepared for cruelty, but nobody speaks. It's a big city; people must learn to mind their own affairs, and besides, they all seem eager to be out of there.

The air feels ever colder. Her skin puckers. Maybe it's the bourbon wearing off, but she's starting to feel less brave when Morley finally appears, striding through the door like he's just come out of the bank. He's so much in his own head that he doesn't look at them as he walks past.

'Let's come back Wednesday for Ladies' Night,' Gloria calls to him. 'Maybe you can dance.'

He spins about and sees her.

'Christ! Have you lost your mind?' As he rushes to her side, his limbs seem unschooled, flailing with none of their familiar discipline. Frantically, he grabs her nightgown and shoves it over her head. She doesn't raise her arms, though, so the gown just flops down across the front of her like an outsize bib.

Then he looks up and sees Attie.

'Hey, slugger,' she says, winking at him.

'What in the hell is going on?' he shouts.

Attie shrugs theatrically and doesn't answer.

Returning his attention to Gloria, he pulls at her nightgown until he's found the sleeves. She lets him work them over her arms. When it comes to getting the rest back on, he tugs and crams the fabric without success, and when Attie steps in to help, he swears at her. Finally, Gloria braces herself against the sides of the chair and lifts herself to let him finish the job.

'I don't know how you got her up to this,' he says to Attie.

'Don't blame her,' Gloria says. 'All she did was keep me company.'

He keeps staring at Attie like he doesn't believe it. Gloria can see that vein on his neck twitching. Then she has a moment of inspiration.

'Attie and I have been talking,' she says. 'About how you two should race.'

Attie looks at her with bewilderment.

'I told you, I'm not racing her,' says Morley. He's still staring at Attie. 'Whatever you're up to, you can go to hell.' Then he turns to Gloria. 'I'm taking you home.'

He reaches for the handles and starts to push, but Gloria has her hand firmly on the brake.

'I think you two should race right now,' she says. 'Here, in front of this place.'

His face screws up in disbelief. 'What are you talking about? I just found you naked in the street. We're going back to the hotel.'

'Then you two should race from here to there,' says Gloria. The moment she speaks the words, the idea grows solid, shining, almost real. 'What do you think, Attie?'

Attie's eyes are all glassy, reflecting neon. 'Oh,' she says, sounding doubtful. But she must have some realization of just how preposterous and perfect a race here and now would be, because she breaks into a smile. 'I think it would be amazing.'

Morley looks at them as if he thought he knew them backward and forward, and now they've turned into utter strangers.

'What do you say?' Gloria asks him. 'Or would you rather go back in there with us?' She nods toward the Apollo.

Morley glances at his watch, then down the hill toward the hotel. It can't be more than 400 metres.

'Fine, let's race,' he says. 'Back to the hotel so I can sleep, and maybe when I wake up, my wife will have stopped being a lunatic.'

He takes off his leather jacket. When he offers it to Gloria, she sets it on her lap and feels its warmth disperse into her thighs.

As if a switch has been flipped, Attie and Morley transform. They stand straighter now, bouncing in place, stretching out their legs. Both of them are wearing running shoes; it seems to be part of distance runners' creed always to have them on, like swordsmen who are never parted from their swords.

'From here to the lobby door?' says Attie.

'On one condition,' says Morley. 'I get a handicap. I'll push Gloria in her chair.'

Attie shakes her head. 'No way. Don't patronize me. Besides, that would just give you an excuse when you lose.'

'Forget it, then,' says Morley. 'I'm not racing.'

Then Gloria has an idea. 'How about this?' she says to him. 'If you push me and Attie wins, we'll go again with Attie pushing me.

If you win the second time, the two of you can call it a draw and forget the whole thing.' She turns to Attie. 'How does that sound?'

Attie considers it. Gloria suspects that normally she wouldn't agree, but then, all three of them have been drinking.

After a time, Attie nods.

'You're both nuts,' says Morley. He grabs hold of the chair's handles, though, and points Gloria toward the hotel. She isn't surprised. He's the one who races shorter distances. He must be confident that he can win in a downhill sprint.

It's almost one-thirty, and the street is deserted. Morley points to a crack in the asphalt and declares it the starting line. Once Attie positions herself behind it, Morley manoeuvres Gloria into a parallel spot in the bike lane. Gloria is already thinking about the second race. She pictures Attie driving her onward, the two of them flying past Morley as his arms pump and his knees churn. She desperately wants Attie to win the first race, just to get that chance.

'I'll be the starter,' Gloria announces. Then, before either of them is ready, she yells out, 'Go!'

She grips the armrests, preparing for the jolt of Morley launching her forward. For a split second, there's nothing, and her heart sinks at the thought that he's backed out. In the corner of her eye, Attie charges ahead. Then there's a lurch forward, and Gloria's roaring down the hill.

Not having anyone to push, Attie keeps her early lead. Gloria hears Morley straining to close the gap, but he can't use his arms to help him run while he's steering the chair, and his top speed appears to be no better than Attie's. Already, the three of them are halfway down the hill. Attie's going to win.

Then he does something different: Gloria feels him release the handles and shove the back of her chair hard. She surges ahead until she's even with Attie. She hears him sprint up behind her, his strides longer now that he isn't holding the chair. Unguided, the chair starts veering toward the curb. She feels him grab the handles for a moment to point her back in the right direction before giving her another shove.

Attie's still even with them, her long hair waving behind her. She glances over at Gloria and grins. Then her mouth flatlines, and she looks down at herself. Gloria sees what has happened: Attie's right breast has moved out of position again. All in one motion, Attie reaches up inside her blouse and pulls out a white pad, the size of an apple but more triangular than round.

'What are you doing?' Morley shouts at her.

The chair shivers as it passes over another crack in the road. A second later, he cries out in pain, and there's the thud of his body hitting the pavement. The sound of his footsteps disappears. Gloria looks back to catch a glimpse of him sprawled on his belly.

She looks over to Attie. She has broken her stride to take Morley in, just for a second, before she returns her gaze to Gloria, who's speeding away down the hill.

They've hit the steep part of the slope, and now Gloria's really moving. She's afraid to touch the brakes. She's afraid to touch the rims when they're spinning at such a pace, roaring like a chariot's wheels. Attie has started after her but hasn't caught up. Gloria hurtles toward the ocean, the tops of the ancient firs in Stanley Park steepling into the sky before her. She's going so quickly, it's like she's in a movie, like she's accelerating into the past, back to a time before the age of the dinosaurs, before the world held animals of any kind, before the birth of the fossil record. Gloria waits and waits for Attie to save her life.

REPORT ON THE BIGFOOT COLLECTIVE

Whoa! Hard act to follow! Thanks, Kaylee and Brayden, for your informative talk on the dangers of karaoke, and thank you, Ms. Lam, for this chance to speak with the class. In our presentation, Eddie and I would like to tell you about the Bigfoot collective.

I see eyebrows rising. Is the Bigfoot collective an appropriate topic for a civics report? We say yes, because although you may not have heard of the collective, it includes many Bigfoot right here in the forests of Lewis County and the rest of Upstate New York. Are the Bigfoot a topic I'd have chosen on my own? No, they are not. But, as Ms. Lam has told me since assigning Eddie to me as a partner, embracing others' ideas is key to success in the tenth grade, and also in life.

(Ms. Lam, as I write these words, I want you to know that I haven't forgotten your request that we speak from notes instead of reading out our written reports. But the idea of me trying to talk to everyone in complete sentences that I'm making up as I go is literal nightmare fuel, so I'm writing down all the words now, and I'll practise saying them so that in class I seem all witty and natural and not like a control freak having a panic attack.)

First, let's bust a myth: the Bigfoot are not sasquatches. Eddie has explained to me that the sasquatch is a whole other species. The Bigfoot are *homo sapiens*. If this fact feels hard to wrap your head around, I hear you, but go with it. We have a lot to cover, and I don't want to lose marks for running overtime.

Another myth is that the Bigfoot all have big feet. According to Eddie's informant in the collective, the Bigfoot calling themselves by that name is an inside joke, because their whole lifestyle is about leaving hardly any footprint on the Earth. Those Bigfoot: what a bunch of comedians!

So, who are the Bigfoot, if not sasquatch with big feet? According to Eddie, they're people from all walks of life who are joined by a deep desire for peace and quiet.

I can hear some of you saying to me, 'Ava, I like peace and quiet. Am I a Bigfoot?' Well, that depends. Do you live in a house? Do you buy stuff? If you do, then sorry, you're not a Bigfoot, because the Bigfoot are against property and possessions. They sleep in lean-tos, and they own as little as possible, sharing what they have. They believe in looking after the land and considering their actions' effects on future generations.

They don't have kids, though. The whole purpose of being a Bigfoot is to remove yourself from a system of endless economic growth, unfair inheritance laws, and environmental debauchery. Yes, I just said 'debauchery,' but I'm not trying to show off: *debauchery* was a Word of the Day in March, and it was Jonah who chose it, not me.

Another myth about the Bigfoot is that sometimes in the woods at night, you can hear their cries. Eddie's informant says the Bigfoot never raise their voices. When you're trying to avoid the rest of humanity, you don't call attention to yourself. Also, the Bigfoot don't like noise. Maybe the thing they hate most about people is our racket: the fireworks, loudspeakers, leaf-blowers, and car engines. The Bigfoot believe that a noisy person is an aggressive person. They say that raising your voice only puts you in a bad light. You hear that, Ms. Lam? Ha, just kidding. You're pretty quiet, for a teacher.

If this were a normal presentation – you might even say, if it were a *fair* presentation – it would now be Eddie's turn to speak. I bet you'd like to hear from him, right? He's kind of a mystery man – an *enigma*, to use a Word of the Day from February. (Great choice, Jasmine!) Eddie's the county record-holder in the discus, but he never talks about it. Nowadays, he doesn't talk at all, because, as I learned right after Ms. Lam made us partners for this report, he has taken a vow of silence. Do you know anyone else who has taken a vow of silence? I do not. Are fifteen-year-olds even *allowed* to take vows of silence? In my family, giving someone the silent treatment gets you grounded if my stepmom finds out. Is it fair that Eddie has taken a vow of silence the same week he was due to give a report with a partner whose grade depends partly on Eddie's ability to step up? No comment.

At this point, let me call on Eddie to join me at the front of the class so I can make an announcement for him. I told him that he should make it himself, but I appreciate how announcements are tricky when you've taken a vow of silence. I requested that he at least write out his announcement for me to read, but he said that he trusts me to find the right words. Okay, he didn't say it; he wrote it on a notepad. Why didn't he just message me? you ask. Turns out he's sworn off using his phone, too.

(At first, Ms. Lam, I thought that Eddie claiming to have given up his phone might be a way of forcing me to work with him in person. But that would be weird, because, as I mentioned to you the other day, he and I have barely spoken since he and his mom moved off our block in Grade 5.)

Okay, so here's Eddie, and here's his announcement: he's a Bigfoot. More accurately, he's an apprentice Bigfoot. I mean, he still lives at home with his mom. Once he's of age, though, he'll move to the woods to join a Bigfoot group he met earlier this spring.

Eddie's Bigfoot identity is why he's given up his phone and taken a vow of silence. You don't have to stop speaking to be a Bigfoot, but I guess he figures that while he's still living among the non-Bigfoot population, he should compensate by being ultra-Bigfoot in other ways.

Now, some of you might be thinking about how Eddie is six-five, how he's the only person in our class with facial hair, and how he has size-fourteen feet. I'm not body-shaming him; he wanted me to mention these things. He knows that he looks like a stereotypical sasquatch – which, I should emphasize, is a figure from the legends of the Sts'ailes people up in Canada that colonizers got excited about and changed around. In other words, the tall, hairy Bigfoot you're picturing is fake, and it's just bad luck that Eddie resembles it.

We're nearly out of time, so we'd better start the Q&A part of our presentation. Eddie can't reply to your questions by speaking, but he can write answers on the board. What would you like to know?

Ms. Lam, this part of our presentation stresses me out. Someone might ask why Eddie feels compelled to tell everyone he's a Bigfoot, or they might ask why they should believe in the Bigfoot at all. These are fair questions, and I don't want him to be humiliated.

I guess you've made an impression on me this year, because I can hear your voice in my head, encouraging me to give him advice on how to manage the situation. After all, don't I handle people just fine when they make fun of me for using big words? Honestly, though, the only way I cope is by telling myself that a teenager's miseries are *evanescent* (Word of the Day, March 21) and that eventually I'll be a famous novelist whose writing about my high school tormentors is the sole surviving record of them on Earth. I remember you saying to me last fall that you didn't find your people until college. I take comfort from that.

So please don't think I'm blaming this Eddie situation on you. But I still don't understand why you insisted on him and me working together, even after he told me about his vow of silence and wanting to do our report on the Bigfoot. I mean, I believe what you said about the partner assignments being random. Were you listening to me, though, when I explained that Eddie and I haven't been friends since the fifth grade? That we haven't spoken since then? It feels like you've done something shitty.

So now I've written 'shitty,' and if I turn this in, I'll probably be suspended. Also, this report's way over the word limit. But I want to tell you everything.

For example, about Eddie and me. Yesterday at lunchtime, after he handed me a bunch of pages he'd written on the Bigfoot, I asked him what evidence we could include to prove they exist. I said that maybe he could introduce me to his informant.

In response, he scribbled on his notepad: 'The Bigfoot won't talk with an outsider. Not unless the person wants to join them.'

I admitted that I didn't want to do that.

Neither of us mentioned that we hadn't spoken in five years. Eddie didn't ask how my dad was, and I didn't ask about his mom. I did ask why he'd decided to call himself a Bigfoot when he must know that people will make fun of him, and he told me that it just feels right.

That answer made me jealous. Whenever I consider admitting something personal to someone, I get all twisted up, thinking of the risks. If making a big confession ever just felt right to me, I'd be terrified, because I'd assume that I hadn't properly considered the angles.

I got even more jealous of Eddie when I read in the pages he'd given me that he felt welcomed by the Bigfoot. Ms. Lam, I've never felt welcomed by anybody. You know I don't have friends at school. Online, I lurk in writing groups, but they're too intimidating for me to post my stories. Even when I get bused across the county for gifted-kids days, I'm the odd one out. I'm probably the only student in the program who isn't at the top of my class; the only one who doesn't even hand in homework half the time, because my brain's too squirrelly. I do like writing stories, but even then, I can never tell where to stop. With essays,

I have so many ideas that I can't get them down properly, which is ironic, because when I'm with the gifted kids, the one thing that makes me stand out is my vocabulary. All the words in my head only make talking harder, though. Like, do I say *crepuscular* or *twilight*? *Corporeal* or *embodied*? You've said that we have a Word of the Day in civics class because a person's vocabulary limits what they can understand about the world, but in my experience, it doesn't matter how many words you know if you can't decide on the right ones at the right time.

Giving the report would be easier if I could just read out Eddie's account of the Bigfoot and leave things there. It's only a random list of facts, though. So yesterday, I invited him to work with me at my house after school like you suggested. I didn't really want to spend time with him, but I decided to follow your advice to the letter. That way, if the report turns into a train wreck, you can't blame me.

He showed up at four, while my dad and stepmom were still at work. I hadn't told them that Eddie was coming over – I worried it would make them feel weird, for reasons I don't need to get into right now – and I figured that if we finished fast, he could leave before they returned. After he sat down across the kitchen table from me, though, he just stared in every direction. His gawking made me think twice about all the things in the house: the espresso maker, the water cooler, the Roomba recharging in the corner, the fridge covered in yellow Post-its like it was doing its best imitation of Big Bird, the hutch full of my great-grandmother's dishware, the matching throw pillows on the sofa, the recliner draped in my stepmom's favourite wool blanket, the ottoman piled high with magazines, the shelves stuffed with books. If you'd asked me an hour earlier to describe the scene, I'd have called it the picture of coziness. Now, reflecting on Eddie's new Bigfoot identity, I worried that the place looked to him like a horror show.

Sure enough, he wrote on his notepad: 'I don't remember you having so much stuff.'

My cheeks burned. I wanted to tell him that we need the water cooler because the tap water tastes funny. We need our popcorn maker because air-popping is healthier than oil. Those books on the shelves: Ms. Lam, you'll know better than anyone how awful it would be to get rid of books.

Then I thought of the apartment building where Eddie and his mother live now. I imagined him sleeping in a windowless room that barely fits his bed. I pictured him doing his homework on a rickety table. I had the idea that his mother, who can't afford much, might not like her kid giving up all his possessions.

'What does your mom think of you dropping out and moving to the woods?' I asked.

He shrugged.

'You really don't care about college anymore?' I said.

He shrugged again.

I sighed. 'Sorry, I don't get it.'

Looking annoyed, he wrote: 'Ms. Lam gets it. Talk to her.'

The words hit me like a slap. I'd always assumed that I was the only one who talks with you about personal matters. The idea that Eddie does, too, made me sick. Suddenly, I couldn't handle another minute with him.

'You know, maybe we don't need to work together in person,' I said. 'I can finish the report using your notes.'

He looked confused. 'You want me to leave?' he wrote.

'I'm just saying, you don't need to stick around.'

His look turned darker. 'Thanks,' he wrote. Then he got up and walked out of the kitchen.

I should have said sorry. Instead, I listened to him put on his shoes in the entranceway. He paused for a second, like he was waiting for me to speak. I was still angry with him, though, for making me feel like just another teenager desperate for your attention, so I didn't say a word, and he left.

After dinner, I wrote down everything you've just read. Not exactly report material, is it? But I wanted you to know what a horrible person I am. No wonder I don't have friends. Even when Eddie and I hung out together as little kids, he probably only did it for the company.

Back then, Eddie said that he liked spending time with me because when he was by himself at home, his mom yelled at him a lot. Whenever I was at their place, she didn't yell once; she just had a loud voice. He called it yelling, though, and he was always suggesting that we go outside. In the fall, we made leaf piles. In the winter, we built snow forts to defend ourselves against teenage gangs who roamed around in Eddie's head. In the summer, we explored the creek behind our houses. We weren't allowed to play in it during any other season, because at some point before we were born, a boy had drowned there. In the summer, though, the water was only ankle-deep and clogged with cattails. We'd hunt frogs or lie still on the bank, hoping for dragonflies to land on us. The summer before the fifth grade, Eddie showed up at my house almost every day, wanting me to join him down there. I always went, even when I didn't feel like it, because he never asked anything else of me, and he seemed happy for me to sit and read a book while he splashed around in his bare feet, turning over rocks to see what lay beneath. I loved that creek, but Eddie loved it more.

Sometime in July, my dad mentioned that the woodlot behind our house was about to be developed into a new neighbourhood. They planned to bury the creek. When I told Eddie, he wanted to go there right away, as if a construction crew might have already arrived and we could stop them, but when we got there, the place was the same as always. Then Eddie announced that he had a plan. The two of us would dam the creek. We'd flood the whole area, so that beavers would come to live there, and the town wouldn't be able to build anything because of them.

I didn't tell him that there was too little water to start a flood. I didn't say that the town wouldn't care about beavers. Instead, I just let myself enjoy how the plan made my brain light up. It always gets a bigger buzz from crazy possibilities than from ordinary life. Maybe that's why, when Eddie told me this week that he's a Bigfoot, I didn't laugh in his face.

Back then, we spent more time building the dam than you'd expect from a pair of ten-year-olds. For a week, we weaved together dead branches, adding things we found abandoned in the woodlot: a canvas tarp, a milk crate, an old Goodyear tire. We packed mud into the spaces between them. One morning, we showed up to find the dam built up further than how we'd left it the previous day, the little pool upstream nearly knee-high, and Eddie said it must have been beavers, before admitting that he'd come back after dinner to do more work.

I told him he'd done a great job, but the truth is that I was worried. Working on the dam, he seemed driven by an energy that wasn't in his control. I've read on the internet that beavers can't stand the sound of running water. The noise will keep them adding to their dams all day and night. That summer, there wasn't enough water in the creek to make even a gurgle, but Eddie sure acted like he heard one.

When I first told my dad what Eddie and I were doing, he laughed and said that if the creek flooded the backyard, he'd finally have the swimming pool he wanted. Then he turned serious and asked how Eddie was.

'Same as always,' I said. But I was thinking about that energy in him.

'His mom just lost her job,' my dad said. 'Eddie might – ' He stopped himself.

'Might what?' I asked.

'Never mind,' he said. 'Just be patient with him, okay? Not everybody has it as good as you do.'

I nodded, having no clue what being patient with Eddie would mean. He was so quick to make decisions; he always seemed to know his own mind in a way that felt miraculous to me.

The next afternoon, Eddie and I turned up at the creek to find that our dam was gone. The milk crate had been smashed to pieces. The tire lay twenty yards downstream. The branches were scattered on the bank, and the little pool had drained away.

Eddie's face went red. His eyes welled up. He jammed his hands into his pockets like he was afraid of what they'd do.

I almost told him that it didn't matter, that we'd rebuild. I stopped myself, though, because I realized that rebuilding wasn't what I wanted. The dam had been Eddie's thing, not mine. Seeing it demolished, I suddenly knew this fact to be true, and I felt a wave of anger at him for drawing me into his fantasy.

After a time, he went to gather an armful of branches from the bank. I watched him set them back in the middle of the creek. Then he turned to look at me.

'Aren't you going to help?' he said.

'Someone will only wreck it again,' I replied.

He gave a little nod, as if he'd been expecting me to let him down. Instead of saying anything, he went and rolled the tire back to the same spot where we'd placed it together. When he spoke next, he didn't look me in the eye.

'Did you know that after we moved here, my mom made a deal with your dad?' he said. 'So I could have a friend.'

A sick feeling welled up in me – the same feeling as when, this week, he told me that he'd talked with you.

'They didn't make any deal,' I said.

'She told him that you could come over whenever you like, and she'd watch you.'

'That's not a deal. She was just being nice.'

He shook his head. 'You don't know her.'

The conversation went something like that, anyhow. It was a long time ago. But I've thought a lot about it, because it was the last conversation that Eddie and I ever had as friends. I left him working on the dam, and when I got home, I couldn't bring myself to ask my dad about any deals he might have made with Eddie's mom.

Why have I told you all this, Ms. Lam? Does it explain why Eddie and I aren't close anymore? It's easier to say that he moved across town a few weeks later and never invited me over. In the fall, a crew turned up to bury the creek, and I never asked Eddie back to our place either, because I didn't want him to see what they'd done.

Yesterday, as soon as he left my house, I knew that I didn't have a good reason to be upset with him. It wasn't until this morning, though, that I felt properly *conciliatory* (April 11). I decided to apologize and ask if he might give working together another try. But he wasn't in class, so I made a plan to stop by his place after school.

When I texted my stepmom to let her know, she wrote back: *Eddie who lived down the block?*

Is that a problem? I wrote.

No, she replied. *Be home by five.*

Eddie and his mom live on the east side, over in Heron Grove. That's the name of the old three-storey apartment buildings there, all clustered around a gravel parking lot full of potholes. People call it Heroin Grove. Even though you've only been in town a year, Ms. Lam, you might have figured out that in these parts, there are two kinds of families. There are the ones in which the kids' lives are loaded up with sports, clubs, vacations, and new clothes for each new school year, and the parents are doctors, or teachers, or software engineers working remotely for big companies. Families like mine. Then there are the families in Heron Grove. The parents have jobs at the gas bars and fast-food restaurants, or they clean floors or drive the garbage truck, or they don't work at all. The kids don't join clubs or teams. They sit in class looking kind of sleepy, like school's a break from bigger dramas playing out elsewhere in their lives. At least, that's how Eddie has seemed to me, the past few years.

On my way to his place, I went by the high school. I'd seen him there other evenings, all by himself, throwing his discus around the infield. This time, he wasn't anywhere in sight, but Coach Johnson stood by the track with his stopwatch dangling from his neck, watching a bunch of girls run laps. I have to admit, Ms. Lam, I'm not a big fan of Coach Johnson. For one thing, I once heard him make a joke about you to some boys in class. I won't repeat it here, but I was so mad that I couldn't think of anything to say until later. (I won't tell you what reply I settled on either, because it involves more words that would get me suspended. *Esprit d'escalier*: remember in October, when it was my turn to choose the Word of the Day, and I chose *esprit d'escalier*, and Daisy complained that it was two words, maybe three, and it wasn't English, and you told her not to be pedantic? That's when you became my favourite teacher.) I called out hello, and Coach Johnson just stared at me, probably trying to remember my name. He only pays attention to the kids on his teams. When I asked him if he'd seen Eddie, he shook his head and scowled.

'He could be at home, packing,' he said.

'Packing for what?' I said.

He scowled harder. 'Are you friends with him?'

I wasn't sure how to answer. I thought that it might seem weird for someone who wasn't Eddie's friend to be asking about him.

'We're doing a presentation,' I said finally.

Coach Johnson looked unimpressed. 'You know he's taken a vow of silence?'

I nodded.

'His teachers keep ragging on me like it's my fault,' he said. His eyes narrowed. 'He tell you why he took it?'

When I shook my head, he looked disappointed.

'He tell you what he's decided to do next year?' he asked.

I shook my head again, and his face softened, like he'd realized that he and I were in the same basic boat – one without Eddie as a passenger.

'Yeah, well, if you see him, remind him that he owes me an explanation,' he said.

Before I left the school, I checked the staff lot for your car. I remembered you once telling me that you like to work in your classroom after everyone has left for the day. You said that it's better than sitting alone at home. Tonight, though, your car wasn't there, and when I went by the classroom, all the lights were off.

Once I got to Heron Grove, I realized that I didn't know which apartment Eddie's was. I didn't even know which building he lived in. There was nobody to ask, and I was too big a coward to start randomly knocking on doors, so I climbed the stairs of the nearest building and walked along the breezeway at the top, hoping to hear the voice of Eddie's mom inside one of the apartments.

As I passed the doors, I heard a lot of things: a man yelling at someone to leave their sister alone; the sizzle of grease in a fry pan; a TV blaring about the election. I went along the whole flyway and half of the next one down before I saw a pair of enormous sneakers sitting on the mat outside a door. I picked up one of them and checked the tag on the tongue. Size fourteen. When I knocked, a woman inside called out for me to enter. She sounded a lot like Eddie's mom.

The door opened into a tiny living room. The curtains had been drawn, but they didn't reach all the way across the window. The only furniture was a ratty, floral-print loveseat. The rest of the room was filled with cardboard boxes that had words like 'BEDRM' and 'JUNK?' scrawled on their sides. Eddie's mother stood among them. I hadn't seen her since the fifth grade, but other than the fact that she'd cut her hair into a bob, she looked the same: short and thin, like Eddie before his growth spurt. She even wore the same heart-shaped earrings and salmony lipstick that I remember from back then. Judging by her face, she had no clue who I was, so I said hello and told her I was Ava Shapin, from Juniper Street.

'Ava,' she exclaimed, breaking into a smile. 'You're all grown up.' She still had a pretty loud voice.

When I asked her if Eddie was home, her smile vanished.

'He makes it hard, not using his phone, right?' she said. 'He's been out in the woods since lunch. I know it's a school day, but he needed a break.' She spoke the words like I'd made some objection. 'What time is it? He said he'd be back by four.'

While she checked her phone, I stared at the boxes. 'You're moving?' I said.

She nodded. 'Denver. New job.'

I don't know why the words hit me so hard. I guess I'd assumed that she and Eddie were headed to another place in town.

'But there's still a month of school,' I said.

'I start work on Monday,' she said. 'Eddie will stay here to train with Coach Johnson until the fall. Then he has a scholarship at a boarding school in Albuquerque. He didn't tell you?'

I shook my head.

'They have an awesome throws program,' she said. 'Eddie wants to get into a top college, and the discus is his best chance.' She must have sensed my lack of enthusiasm, because she added, 'A college like your dad went to, right? Anyway, a change of scenery will do Eddie good. You know he's had troubles? He's spent a lot of time with the school psychologist.'

I didn't know what to say. She hadn't seen me since the fifth grade; she must have understood that Eddie and I weren't friends.

'He's worried about not knowing anyone at the new school,' she said. 'But it couldn't be much worse than here, could it? I mean, what do kids say about him?'

I hesitated. Eddie keeps to himself so much. Whenever there's a morning announcement that he's won gold at another track meet, everyone claps, but nobody cares.

'People admire him,' I said. 'For his – ' I considered how to end the sentence. *Principles? Proficiency? Pertinacity?* Before I could choose, she'd moved on.

'And now he's stopped speaking,' she said. 'He tell you why?'

'Sorry, no,' I replied.

She stared at me for a while. 'Oh, well,' she said finally, looking over at a dinette table covered in shoeboxes. 'You can wait for him here if you like. Are you hungry? I made pasta.'

As she started toward the kitchen, I heard a rumble from outside. It got louder and louder, shaking the apartment. Through the space between the curtains, I could see something in motion: the top of a freight train, running smoothly left to right, looking almost close enough to jump onto. The train took a couple of minutes to pass by, and even once I'd followed Eddie's mom into the kitchen, I could still feel the vibrations.

'Three times a day,' she said. 'And once at night, when you're trying to sleep.'

At this point, Ms. Lam, I should tell you that when Eddie lived on my block, my dad and Eddie's mom went on two dates. Dinner and a movie both times. This was before my dad met my stepmother, before Eddie and I built the dam. Both nights, our parents hired a babysitter to look after the two of us together. Both nights, Eddie and I watched TV, but I couldn't focus on the screen. Would our parents kiss? Get married? I pictured myself as the flower girl and Eddie as the ring bearer.

My dad never told me why a third date didn't happen. The next summer, Eddie's mom lost her job as a receptionist, and our dam got wrecked, and she and Eddie moved to Heron Grove. By then, my dad had started dating my stepmom.

Today, as I sat at Eddie's dinette table and watched his mom slide a plate of spaghetti into the microwave, I thought how this could have been my life, except we'd be at my house right then, with its chef's kitchen and bamboo floor. I wondered if she was thinking the same thing. Maybe she assumed that I'd been the one to keep my dad from going on another date with her. She might blame me for Heron Grove and late-night trains and Eddie's loneliness, the same way that Eddie probably did.

Then I remembered what Eddie had said, all those years ago, about his mom making a deal with my dad, and suddenly the spaghetti felt like a trap. She wanted to keep me there, turn me into Eddie's girlfriend. I remembered something you told me last month, Ms. Lam, after you lent me *Jane Eyre*: that every woman, at one point or another, is expected to rescue a man from himself.

I stood up and said I had to leave.

'Oh, stay a bit longer,' said Eddie's mom. 'He'll be back any minute.'

The pleading note in her voice made me even more desperate to go. A second later, the microwave dinged like the bell at the end of the school day, and it freed me to head for the door.

I was halfway across town when my dad pulled up beside me in his Volvo. He was wearing a jacket and tie, which meant he hadn't yet been home from work, and he waved at me with an annoying look of relief.

'Did Trish order you to hunt me down?' I said. 'I told her where I'd be.' Checking my phone, I saw that she'd texted half a dozen times. 'She thought I was going to get murdered at Heroin Grove, didn't she?'

He laughed, then looked guilty at having done it. 'You shouldn't call it that.'

'You're the one who laughed.' I got into the Volvo and pretended to read my phone, so that we didn't speak again until we'd reached our driveway.

'Will you tell me something?' I said as he turned off the engine. 'Why didn't things work out with you and Eddie's mom?'

'Eddie's mom? Ava, that was years ago.'

'After you stopped dating her, they moved away.'

'Because she lost her job.'

'But what went wrong with you two? Wasn't she nice?'

'Sure she was.' He took a deep breath. 'We weren't a good fit, is all.'

'And Trish was a better one? Why? Because she'd gone to college?'

He put on a hurt look. 'What's got into you?'

'Nothing,' I said. 'I just want to know.'

Inside, Trish was making dinner. She asked why I hadn't replied to her texts, but Dad must have given her some signal, because then she asked in a lighter tone if I was hungry. I said that I wasn't and went upstairs. In my room, I opened my laptop and wrote out everything that had happened: Eddie coming over, the conversation with his mom, the talk with my dad. I wanted to get down all the details for you while they were fresh and true.

It was after nine when Trish knocked on the door to announce that Eddie was downstairs.

'I told him it's too late for visiting, but he claims he just needs a minute,' she said. 'Did he lose his voice? He's writing on a notepad – '

'I'll explain later,' I said.

In the entranceway, Eddie held up a page from his notepad that read: 'Changed my mind. Don't want to tell people I'm a Bigfoot. Not worth it.'

'Yeah, no kidding,' I said. 'Why did it take you so long to figure that out?'

He started to write more before stopping, tearing off the sheet, and slipping it into his pocket. Then his shoulders slumped.

'Never mind,' he said.

His voice was deep, even deeper than I remember it being the few times this year that he's said something in class. It took me a second to realize the significance of him speaking. Then I got the angriest I've felt in a long time.

'Just like that, your vow's over?' I said. 'How long did it last? A week?'

His eyes narrowed. 'You should be glad. Now I can read the report out loud with you.'

'The report that's about how you won't be talking?'

His lips pursed. 'I'll rewrite everything tonight.'

'It won't be the same.'

'You mean it won't be as good. You don't even want to be my partner.'

The words put a knot in my stomach. 'Did Ms. Lam say that?' I meant to sound angry, but my voice came out choked. I couldn't stand the thought of you betraying me like that.

Eddie shook his head. 'She didn't have to say anything.'

Ms. Lam, I'm not stupid. I knew that Eddie and I weren't really arguing about our report. We were arguing about him moving to Heron Grove in the fifth grade.

'You're going to Albuquerque,' I said. 'To some boarding school?'

His eyes went to the floor. 'Don't tell Coach. He thinks I'm still deciding.'

'What about living with the Bigfoot?' I asked.

He glanced back up, as if to see whether I was making fun of him. Honestly, he was right to be suspicious. Part of me felt like saying he needed a better way of dealing with his problems than make-believe. But in that moment, to let him keep pretending that the Bigfoot collective exists felt like the one thing I could do for him.

'It's too bad you're moving,' I said. 'I thought maybe we could start hanging out again.' I don't know what made me say such a thing. I hadn't been thinking it.

Eddie cocked an eyebrow.

'I mean it,' I said, sounding even less believable.

'Yeah, well, I'm here until August,' he replied.

'Then you should come over sometime,' I said. 'We have a swimming pool now.'

'Sure,' he said. 'Sometime.'

There was so much sadness in his voice. I wanted to say: *You're not the only one who's lonely.* I wanted to say: *We could have been brother and sister.* But he just murmured a goodbye and left. We hadn't even decided how to give our report.

Ms. Lam, I don't get you. You laugh at my jokes, you tell me about your life, you seem so kind and trustworthy, and then you sell me out to Eddie by saying I didn't want to be his partner. Or if you didn't say it, you said something that let him put two and two together.

I wonder if you think about me as much as I think about you. Do you spend time remembering how it was when you were my age? The crushes you had, the wild hopes? The difficulty of giving them up, no matter how wrong they were? Do you remember how much you wanted to be somebody other than the person you could feel yourself becoming, a person who might one day find herself grown up and alone in a town far away, renting a tiny house, preparing lesson plans and grading student reports late into the night?

Just now, I took a break from writing this to go for a walk in the woodlot behind my house. There aren't many trees left now, but tonight, whenever the moon slid behind the clouds, the forest seemed limitless. Then, across town, a train whistled. As the sound faded, I swear that I could hear the creek, deep underground, singing in its culvert. I wanted to howl like a wolf. With each step I took, my bare feet sunk into the earth. I could feel them swelling, becoming the biggest feet in the world, the kind that trip you up no matter how careful you are. I wanted to keep walking into the forest, away from Eddie, my family, school. I imagined you out there with me, Ms. Lam, the two of us creating a little Bigfoot collective all our own. But you should never trust your feelings about the woods, not when it's after midnight and the moon is full.

I don't think that Eddie has really made up his mind, Ms. Lam. And now that he's broken his vow of silence, he has nothing to protect him from admitting that he doesn't know what to do.

It's almost six in the morning, I'm back in my room, and I haven't slept. Eddie and I are due to give our presentation in a few hours. I've decided that I'll tell him not to worry: he doesn't have to speak. I'll read out the first pages of this report that's far too long and not much of a report, and then, tonight, I'll return to the woodlot to burn the rest. Or maybe I'll hand in everything to you and see what happens.

I can hear my stepmom downstairs, making her first espresso of the day. She drinks it non-stop because she never gets enough sleep. I never get enough either, but she says I'm too young for coffee. So, school today will last forever. At the start of civics, you'll write the Word of the Day on the board, and as I copy it down, my hands will be trembling at the thought of giving our report. At some point, you'll notice the bags under my eyes like you always do. After class, you'll tell me that you worry about me. I'll say that I'm going to be fine.

And Eddie? He'll be all right, won't he? Ms. Lam, tell me he'll be okay.

YOUR PUPPY MEETS THE WORLD

You've gone and got yourself a puppy. Great job! At this moment in your life and world history, it seems one of the saner, more straightforward things to do: an investment in the future, a gift to yourself. At the same time, if you think your puppy is coming to you fully prepared for new adventures, you're dead wrong.

Have you read the work of Dr. Sophia Yin, author of *Perfect Puppy in 7 Days*? Don't worry if you haven't, nobody has time for reading nowadays, but it would help you to understand some things. You'd know that the world will alarm your puppy. The world will frighten him. More often than not, the world will lead to your puppy's overarousal.

If your puppy's first experiences are negative, they could ruin him forever. Watching your puppy's fight-or-flight response get triggered may be, in the moment, super cute – who doesn't want to see your puppy bare his tiny widdle teeth or tuck his adorable tail between legs you just want to put in your mouth? – but the long-term payoff will be a disaster. We're talking growling, lunging, barking, and biting. We're talking chewed ottomans, incontinence, and rock-bottom self-esteem. We're talking about you spending the next ten to eighteen years, maybe once a day, saying, 'I'm so sorry, he's never done that before.' Nobody wants that life. As soon as possible, you've got to expose your puppy to diverse new stimuli, and you've got to make it totally fun. With that goal in mind, let's consider a simple set of instructions to help prepare your puppy for the world.

You might think that these steps don't have a climate-crisis level of urgency, but this isn't a situation that you can hope will be fixed by politicians or science or – ha! – the market. You need to handle it yourself. You might also think that completing all the steps isn't a priority like other things in your life right now, things to help make you a happier, more attractive person, but let's face it, you've got years ahead as a work-in-progress. Your puppy's window of opportunity will be closing really soon.

Keep in mind the value of treats. For example, give your puppy a treat every time you introduce him to new kinds of touch. Give him a treat when first handling his ears. Give him a treat when first checking his gums, first opening his eyelids with your fingers, and first clipping his toenails. Also, when first pinching his skin – maybe every time you do that, actually. Give him a treat when first gently tweaking his nose with the tip of a ballpoint pen. Treats will make your puppy look forward to moments of contact in ways I think you'll find affecting.

Introduce your puppy to other kinds of touch. Hug your puppy. Hold your puppy in your lap. Pick up your puppy and cradle him. (To be honest, if you haven't been doing these things already, what is wrong with you?) Put your puppy on his back and scratch his belly. Wipe your puppy with a beach towel like he's a dirty, dirty dog. Hold your puppy upside down. Give your puppy's collar a tug. Grab your puppy by a part of his body. (If you don't know which parts to grab and which to leave alone, what is wrong with you?)

In your puppy's presence, bang some pots and pans. Shake out a blanket. Beat a rug. Sweep and mop your kitchen. I bet it needs doing anyway. Open an umbrella. Bonus points if it's raining; you think your puppy wants to get rained on? Blow up a balloon and rub it against your head, thus acquainting your puppy at the same time with balloons and with static electricity.

It's important for your puppy to feel comfortable around other animals. Introduce him to a pigeon. Introduce him to a squirrel.

Get out of the house for once and introduce your puppy to some alpacas. Introduce him to the cat that keeps crapping in your garden. Introduce him to your college-age children. (I appreciate that you may be withholding this introduction to send the kids a message. You wouldn't need a puppy if they weren't such shits.)

Your puppy should get used to different surfaces. Introduce him to hardwood, cork, concrete, and black ice. Introduce your puppy to sewer grates and manhole covers. Introduce your puppy to muddy lawns and carpets, but not on the same day in that order.

Your puppy should get used to noises. Introduce your puppy to thunder. Introduce your puppy to fireworks. Introduce your puppy to the crying of babies or, as I like to call them, human puppies. Introduce your puppy to alarms and sirens. Introduce your puppy to movie scores by Hans Zimmer. Introduce your puppy to the doorbell ringing, and always be the one who rings it, so that if a neighbour eventually comes by to check on you and rings it while you're inside with your puppy, your puppy will give you a really sweet look of confusion.

Show your puppy trash cans. Show your puppy shopping carts and wheelchairs. Show your puppy skateboards, and take a photo of your puppy on a skateboard. (If you don't post this photo on social media, what is wrong with you?)

Take your puppy to the suburbs. Take your puppy to a shopping mall. Take your puppy to Banana Republic and pick out something nice for yourself. You deserve it! Take your puppy on escalators. Take your puppy for mimosas, but not too many this time. Take your puppy to a police auction and a speed-dating session.

Introduce your puppy to other puppies. Introduce your puppy to adult dogs who like to play. Introduce your puppy to adult dogs who don't like to play and who rebuff your puppy's overtures by feigning interest in other activities.

Expose your puppy to men. Expose your puppy to men with chinstrap beards. Expose your puppy to judgmental men with deep voices and dicey tattoos. Expose your puppy to your ex and insinuate that there's somebody new in the picture. Expose your puppy to people who differ from you culturally. Consider the challenges that this step poses for you, and reflect on your life choices. Expose your puppy to people wearing ball caps. Expose your puppy to people wearing Uggs. Expose your puppy to your co-worker who seems standoffish but could be pretty great if you got to know them and they stopped wearing Uggs. Expose your puppy to binge-watching. Expose your puppy to speed-dating again. Expose your puppy to somebody in an old-age home. As you do, try not to dwell on which of them will outlive the other. Expose your puppy to lines of credit. Expose your puppy to wearing sunglasses when it's cloudy. Expose your puppy to the nice people outside the bar who helped get you into a cab.

Expose your puppy to decluttering. Expose your puppy to the films of Claire Denis. Expose your puppy to zero-hour contracts. Expose your puppy to sleeping in a bed alone. Do not expose yourself to your puppy, or what is wrong with you?

Training a puppy is hard. There will be frustrations. There will be setbacks. Through all the hurdles and difficulties, it's important that you not lose hope in your puppy or yourself, and that you not lose hope in the world. I know you still have hope, in spite of everything that's happened, or else what would you be doing with a puppy?

SOMETHING SOMETHING AISLING MOON

Nessa was sitting in Hadi's car, letting the AC run with the engine off, thinking that if the battery died, it served him right for taking so long in the pharmacy, and surveying the main street of Wiarton, which was nearly deserted even on a sunny summer morning, when whom did she see approaching the discount rack outside the clothing boutique but Aisling Moon? At least, she was pretty sure it was Aisling Moon. The past few years, Nessa had developed a habit, no matter where she found herself, whether on the subway in Toronto or strolling along a Venetian canal on vacation with her mother, of seeing strangers in the distance and mistaking them for Aisling Moon. Sometimes they weren't even women, just smallish men, old-timers with silky white hair and a comportment that recalled the hard-bitten grace she associated with Aisling Moon. Whenever she reported these sightings to Hadi, he accused her of being obsessed with Aisling Moon.

'Aisling Moon, always Aisling Moon! How long will it be before a day goes by without you mentioning Aisling Moon?'

He spoke at least partly in jest, knowing it was hard for Nessa to avoid the topic when she was writing her PhD dissertation on Aisling Moon. Or, rather, on the works of Aisling Moon. Nessa usually made a face when other academics used the name of the author – who was a real person, after all – to stand in for the author's writing, saying, for instance, 'I work on Aisling Moon,' which made it sound as if they weren't literary scholars but chiropractors, and ones with a poor sense of chiropractor-client privilege, overeager to share the fact that they got to crack some serious celebrity back, including the vertebrae of one Aisling Moon.

The idea of Nessa coming across the living embodiment of her doctoral dissertation in Venice had been a stretch, but Wiarton wasn't so implausible as the site of an encounter with Aisling Moon. It was a sweet little town on Georgian Bay, the kind of place that often furnished the setting for stories by Aisling Moon. More to the point, Wiarton was a ten-minute drive from Mar, the village where Moon lived, and if you really burned rubber, it was twenty minutes to Lion's Head, where Moon had grown up, back when she was Aisling McCampbell, back when the world had little inkling that unto it had been born the future Aisling Moon. (Nessa didn't know why she entertained fantasies of travelling back to Lion's Head in the forties and finding Aisling McCampbell as a young woman and getting to know her, but she did, and it bothered her, because time-travel stories didn't really fit with her area of study, being a long way from the kinds of things written by Aisling Moon.) Was it so hard to imagine that sometimes, on days such as this one, Wiarton might be a destination of choice for Nessa's favourite writer, a chance to see if the lake was still there, or just a congenial stop on a drive through lands that, over the past half century, had been transformed from ordinary farms, woodlots, and villages into a place now recognized the world over as the everlasting territory of Aisling Moon?

Hadi didn't like it when Nessa referred to Wiarton as territory, making it sound as though the town was no more than literary real estate belonging to Aisling Moon. He'd grown up in Wiarton, and by his account, the experience hadn't been easy, so that the only thing he claimed to want from the place at this stage of his life was to feel that it had furnished material for his own writing, because he was a poet, and a very good one, but still, in the few interviews he'd given, most of them conducted by fellow graduate students, whenever the topic of his formative years came up, the interviewer inevitably wanted to know whether he'd been influenced by Aisling Moon. Had he read Aisling Moon? Had he met Aisling Moon? Given this pattern of questioning, it seemed bad luck that he'd ended up housemates, besties, and occasional fuck buddies with someone whose sole scholarly commitment was to the writing of Aisling Moon.

'Besties and fuck buddies is fine,' he'd told Nessa, 'so long as you don't expect me to spend the holidays with you and your mother or do anything else that might falsely imply an interest in contracting myself to a second-hand involvement in Aisling Moon.'

He was always like this, cool and standoffish, which was strange, because he was a poet, and along with his proclivity for discoursing on things like boustrophedon and lipograms, Nessa would have expected him to be more forthcoming about matters of the heart, which surely weren't the exclusive domain of Aisling Moon. Instead, he seemed happiest talking shop, even when it involved Nessa's research, though he expressed nothing but disdain for the short stories of Aisling Moon.

'Don't you feel,' he'd once said, 'that all her characters are basically, in the end, versions of Aisling Moon?'

'Basically, in the end,' Nessa had replied, 'we're *all* versions of Aisling Moon.'

Despite Hadi's dislike of Moon, he'd been obliging when it came to giving Nessa rides to Wiarton on weekends, even though his mother and sister had moved away from the town not long after he'd left for university, and even though his sole remaining relative in the place was his father, for whom he betrayed perhaps even less affection than he did for Aisling Moon. His father, who owned Wiarton's only pharmacy, apparently didn't betray much affection for Hadi either; at least the way Hadi told it, that was not because the man disapproved of Hadi's lifestyle, given that he didn't know about the drugs and alcohol, but because, as an undergraduate, Hadi had jumped ship from biochemistry to the slowly leaking dinghy that was English Literature, and because he kept company with people who investigated not cures for cancer or compostable plastics but Aisling Moon. Nessa had met Hadi's father only twice, and briefly on each occasion, but now that she thought of it, she was struck that he probably saw her as symbolizing everything distasteful about his son's life, and she wondered if this might be why Hadi kept bringing her to Wiarton, not just because, as she kept impressing on him, she was jonesing for a meet-cute with Aisling Moon.

Over the past two years, various individuals, some of them good friends and some of them people she'd met minutes earlier at parties, had suggested to her that she consider developing an interest in authors other than Aisling Moon. The only time she'd taken the suggestion seriously was at a book launch in Toronto the previous fall, when it had been proposed that she take a look at the work of Michael Ondaatje, but the suggestion had been made by Ondaatje, who seemed biased, and who was also, no matter how many good things one could say about the man and his books, no Aisling Moon.

As Nessa stared at the woman checking out dresses that nobody else had wanted to buy all summer, she started to doubt whether it was actually Aisling Moon. Exiting the car seemed the way to know for sure, and Nessa needed to move fast if she was going to have a chance, but she hesitated, daunted by the possibility that she was about to meet Aisling Moon. What did you say to Aisling Moon? Maybe, after all of Nessa's yearning for this moment, it wasn't right to meet her, not if Nessa aspired to be a proper literary critic, someone who wouldn't let her personal feelings about authors impede her assessments of their work, someone who could stay objective and speak the unvarnished truth about literature by anybody, whether some anonymous medieval shepherd or, well, Aisling Moon. But what the hell; how often did you sit in a car and see Aisling Moon?

She opened the passenger door as quietly as she could, keen not to spook Aisling Moon. Jesus, what was she thinking; it wasn't a deer, it *was* Aisling Moon. And oh my God, it really was Aisling Moon. As the woman stood at the discount rack, rubbing the sleeve of a gingham dress between her thumb and forefinger, Nessa could see the piercing blue eyes and cocked eyebrow that she had, some time ago, come to think of as a distinguished combination, because anyone lucky enough to have them thereby looked rather like Aisling Moon.

Unsure of what her opening move would be, Nessa decided just to walk up and improvise her first-ever words to Aisling Moon. It still seemed unfathomable that Moon could be standing there, bargain-hunting for wardrobe refreshers, living an ordinary life, or at least one as ordinary as life could be if you were Aisling Moon.

'Excuse me,' said Nessa, 'but are you Aisling Moon?'

'Aisling Moon?' replied Aisling Moon. 'Fucksake, do I *look* like Aisling Moon?'

As she said it, she winked, and though her choice of phrasing had been unexpected, her eyes shone exactly like the all-observant eyes of Aisling Moon.

'Well yes, a little,' said Nessa, winking back and trying for the same ironic tone that had just been modelled for her by the one true Aisling Moon.

'Yeah, I know, I'm fucking with you,' said Aisling Moon. 'You're the third tourist this week to tell me I look like Aisling Moon.'

'Wait,' said Nessa, 'are you saying you aren't Aisling Moon?'

Before there was time for an answer, Hadi called out a greeting that seemed intended less for Nessa than for the woman, who, with each passing second, began to fill out around the middle, and whose hair began ever so slightly to darken, looking less and less like Aisling Moon's.

'Hadi!' said the woman, and suddenly Nessa felt that this person had sure as hell better *not* be Moon, because Nessa didn't think that any part of her and Hadi's relationship – not the friendship, the housemateship, or the fuckbuddyship – could survive the discovery that all this time, he'd been on a first-name basis with Aisling Moon.

'Hey, Mrs. Irvine,' said Hadi, going to hug her, and now Nessa didn't know what she'd been thinking, so little did the woman actually resemble Aisling Moon.

'Hadi, you're so grown up, I barely recognized you,' said the woman who was now very obviously not Aisling Moon. 'Did you know,' she said, turning to Nessa, 'that this young man once wrote the best high school essay I ever graded – and the subject, as a matter of fact – '

'Let me guess,' said Nessa with a scowl, 'it was Aisling Moon.'

'Yes, Aisling Moon! Hadi, would you believe that this young woman just mistook me for Aisling Moon?'

'Would *you* believe that she's writing a PhD dissertation on Aisling Moon?' said Hadi, appearing eager to divert attention from what Mrs. Irvine had just revealed about his secret history with Aisling Moon.

'A whole dissertation on her,' said Mrs. Irvine in wonder, as if she figured you could get, at most, a chapter from the topic, maybe two if you considered the influence of Shakespeare on Aisling Moon. 'In my day,' she said, 'it wasn't an option to study Canadian literature, much less Aisling Moon.'

'Mrs. Irvine,' said Hadi, 'I'd love to chat, and I appreciate, honestly, what you said about my paper on Aisling Moon. But, in fact, Nessa here has been keen to meet her, and I've just found out from my father that tonight we're going to be having drinks at his place with, drum roll please – '

'For Christ's sake,' said Nessa, 'don't tell me – '

Hadi broke into a crooked grin and nodded, triumphantly mouthing the paired words of confirmation, somehow as startling as they were familiar: *Aisling Moon.*

You've been selling drugs to Aisling Moon for forty years. That's what you say to people when the chance presents itself to you. It's a violation of the pharmacist's code for you to tell people she's a customer, but you say she probably wouldn't mind, because you don't identify which drugs have been involved, and anyhow, the joke is one that she herself first made to you.

You were surprised, the first time she turned up at the store, because she doesn't live in Wiarton and there's a perfectly serviceable pharmacy in Mar. You aren't a fan of that place yourself, because its inventory doesn't match yours, and because the owner always calls you Mr. Nazem, knowing very well it's your first name, not your last, and knowing well enough, too, that the nickname annoys the hell out of you. In fact, you wonder whether it was the man's assholery that brought Moon's business to you. It wasn't, however, her stated reason, the first time she approached you. Just back from a trip to Australia, voice gravelly from strep throat, she explained that she'd found herself saddled by a certain renown due to writing books, an outcome that was fine and lucky in its way but sometimes inconvenient, and although she knew that pharmacists were supposed to be discreet, she thought it best, to safeguard her privacy, if she were to have prescriptions filled outside of Mar, in Wiarton, by you.

You swore never to betray her.

You must have promised something similar to Mama on your wedding day. You once told me that she and you exchanged no vows, just repeated three times that you accepted each other, but I bet the imam at least wangled a promise to be faithful out of you. You must have done some thinking on the promise – if not that day, then later. You must have felt like shit about yourself.

How many times did you cheat on Mama before she caught you? You made it seem like you were the virtuous one by agreeing to couples counselling. Mama didn't want Nabila and me to know that the two of you were going, but you told us anyhow, as if expecting us to praise you. I wonder, though: Did anything the counsellor say get through to you? I guess there was the one time, after I walked in on Mama shouting at you, that you explained to me how, according to the counsellor, when you're fighting with your spouse, they're liable to fly into a rage if they hear themselves being described by you.

'You should always start your sentences with "I," not "You,"' you told me, in a tone apparently intended to suggest hard-earned wisdom, though to me you just sounded smug. 'Explain your feelings and how things seem to you.' You gave me this advice like it was the secret to a happy marriage, like you and Mama weren't in the process of drafting a separation agreement.

Now, there you are, still living in that rinky-dink house, the guardian of a family history that I doubt anybody treasures, except maybe you. It breaks my heart a little, the thought that after everything we went through there, the house and its memories, its trove of knickknacks that never became heirlooms, might mean something to you. Maybe they don't, though, and you just can't be bothered to move, because it would inconvenience you. You certainly haven't done anything to maintain the property. As Nessa and I approach the front door, the paving stones are cracked, the lawn's grown shaggy, and the shingles are so curled that a decent storm could bring the roof down on you. Hardly the home of someone who cares about built form, yet one night this April, you called me, sniffling away tears, because you'd turned on the TV news to see the Notre-Dame cathedral in flames, and though you'd never visited the place, you said that such a disaster befalling something so beautiful struck at the very core of you. Your idea of yourself and the person I take you to be always seem so far apart.

You open the door even before we reach the porch, and I don't want to think that you've been standing there awhile, waiting to greet us, nothing better to do. Your bald head shines in the evening light, the wound on the crown exposed in order to foster healing. You're following the doctor's orders, leaving that patch of flesh uncovered, though it must embarrass you. I try to avoid staring, not just because it hurts to think of you undergoing an operation, but because you've told me a few times lately that a susceptibility to melanoma is something I might get from you. You've said it out of care, I know, but each time, I've heard you laying down a curse. It's a relief that I'm not expected to ask about the wound or show concern for you. You've downplayed it, so I've downplayed it. You've just called it a growth, so I've done the same.

Once Nessa and I are inside, Nessa hugs you, even though she barely knows you.

'You've arrived before our guest of honour,' you say. 'Let's sit in the living room, and I'll get something to drink for you.'

You look surprised when Nessa hands you the box of caramels she insisted on bringing. She seemed so pleased with herself when she told me they were halal that I didn't have the heart to say it doesn't matter with you. You take them and thank her. You don't mention your diabetes. You do say she can keep her shoes on inside the house, which was never once, in eighteen years of my living here, an option you presented to me.

In the living room, Nessa and I sit on the sofa across from you. You've changed something about the room, but I can't put my finger on it. Your eyes flit nervously between us and the window, keeping an eye out, I guess, for Aisling Moon. You've already forgotten about our drinks.

'You want to dig into the caramels?' Nessa says, hinting to you how hospitality is supposed to work. You shake your head and say you'd rather save them for later.

Could the idea of hosting a famous writer be unsettling you? You seemed so happy when I asked you for the favour. I knew agreeing was a big deal for you, since you and Moon aren't exactly chums, but the request didn't appear to bother you. You looked pleased to do something for me, as happy as I was to do something for Nessa, easy with the idea of making the call and issuing the invitation, especially when I said it could just be drinks.

You aren't usually one to be nervous. I used to wish that your self-confidence was something I'd learn from you. You were so impatient with my lack of eye contact, my stuttering speech. You, who were always so sure of yourself, knowing everything and everyone, claiming to possess more local secrets than Wiarton's three doctors combined, because they each served a mere third of the town, while you served all of it, and plenty of folks clammed up around their physicians, holding them in too high regard to be forthcoming, while you were just a guy from Iran with a charming smile and the good business sense to put on a sympathetic face when people started unburdening themselves. You had the sense, too, to keep things to yourself, letting details slip out only at dinner years later, once the person had died or moved out of town and, as far as you were concerned, released you of your obligation. You never told us anything about Aisling Moon.

Your anxiety must be obvious even to Nessa, because when she addresses you, she does so in a soothing way that I wouldn't expect from her right now, not when her own nerves must be fraying.

'You don't know how much it means to me that you arranged this,' she says. 'I hope it's not an inconvenience to you.'

'No, not at all,' you reply, 'I'm very happy to do it for you.'

'I didn't realize,' says Nessa, 'that Aisling Moon was a friend of yours.'

You give a little smile. 'You know, I wouldn't quite say we're friends. When someone does business with you for a few decades, though, they get to know you. You maybe feel a closeness to them.'

'You feel close to Aisling Moon?' I say. There's an unintended harshness in my voice, and I cringe at how easily the old knee-jerk teen contempt returns, but it has never much fazed you. You seem to accept such moods as the price of having a son.

'You think that's a strange thing to say?' you ask, still smiling. 'I suppose it's not the closeness of friends – not like the two of you.' You look at me as if you have me all figured out, as if you know about the on-again, off-again mess of my life, not only with Nessa but in all things, and then you turn to her, apparently happy to leave me aside. You have more to say about your close-ness to Moon, I can tell, but I don't want to listen.

'Sorry,' I say, rising, 'but I get this uncontrollable need to use the little boys' room whenever the talk turns to Aisling Moon.'

'It's true,' says Nessa with a laugh, 'tonight's going to be hard on you.'

You laugh, too, as if you find nothing more hilarious than the thought of my incontinence.

Upstairs, your bedroom door is closed, which is unlike you. I don't know what compels me to open it and walk in, but I do, and right away I'm hit by the scent of aftershave, work sweat, the smell of you. I keep on going, inspecting the room for traces of you. Your laundry hamper's full, the bed's unmade, and a thin film of dust covers the surfaces. Still sitting atop your dresser, after all these years, are the mortar and pestle I made from clay in Grade 3 for you.

You must be getting sloppy as you near retirement, because you spent years hectoring us not to waste electricity, and now the light in the en suite bathroom has been left on. As I go to turn it off, I glimpse myself in the mirror, and for a second, I can't help it, I picture my head gone bald and my eyes pinched by crow's feet as pronounced as yours. You were forty-five when I was born, and I hope I have a long time yet before I turn into you, but already I can see how it will work, like something you orchestrated a long time ago.

Then I spot the second toothbrush in the cup, nestled next to yours.

The anger that swells in me would frighten you. I tell myself to relax, to act like you. You wouldn't like what I do next, though: I reach down to press my thumb against the bristles of each brush in turn, and I find they're both wet. Not a usual one and a spare, then, but two people's – his and yours.

I go to the closet next, where, sure enough, I find clothes that don't belong to you. You've let him, whoever he is, use Mama's side.

This time, then, it's not just a fling with a cottager or a bachelor farmer who hit it off with you. It's been almost six years since we left you here, and I guess the statutory waiting period has ended, so that the house can finally be given over to whoever's with you.

Downstairs, there's still no sign of Aisling Moon.

'Has she come over here before?' Nessa asks you.

You say she hasn't, and then, for some reason, you admit to inviting her today only because I asked you. After this confession, I expect Nessa to say that I never should have made such a request, but instead she just frowns at you.

'You think maybe we should call her?' she says. 'You know, to make sure she's all right?'

You reply that you don't have Moon's number here at home.

'You have it at the store, though?' Nessa says. 'We could go in with you.'

You seem to consider it but shake your head.

'You might wonder how I've suddenly gained compunctions,' you say, 'but I worry she'd think me too persistent – '

'Oh yes, of course,' says Nessa, 'that's very right of you.'

'You know she's not really coming,' I hear myself declare.

You and Nessa turn to me with a shared look of bemusement.

'You never actually invited her, did you?' I go on. 'You just said you did so you could get us over here. You're always complaining that I never come by.'

You look at me like I'm crazy, and it's true, I don't have a shred of evidence to back me up, at least not beyond the indisputable absence of Aisling Moon.

'She could be sick,' says Nessa, sounding uneasy, 'or she might have a flat tire, or she could have forgotten where you – '

'You don't have to make excuses for him,' I say. 'You see what you've done, Baba? You think it's funny, playing with Nessa's feelings?'

Your eyebrows arch. 'What's gotten into you?'

My breathing comes fast, and it only gets worse when I consider the likelihood that at any second, the doorbell will ring, and standing on the porch with a modestly priced but thoughtfully chosen bottle of wine will be Aisling Moon.

'I think I'll go outside to keep watch,' says Nessa, getting up and heading for the door, 'and you two can talk among yourselves.'

You stand, too, and start to apologize for me, but Nessa says it's fine and leaves. My eyes travel over everything in the room but you. You're starting to say something when I finally realize what's different about the place: the framed photographs of our family that used to sit on the bookshelves and mantelpiece have disappeared.

'You got rid of our photos?' I exclaim.

Your expression turns sheepish, which makes it worse. I would have preferred a front, a lie, something to let me stay furious with you.

'You shouldn't take it the wrong way,' you tell me. 'Every day, I think about Nabila and you.'

'You don't think about Mama, though,' I say, pouncing. 'Your family doesn't include her anymore. You're angry with her for changing her name back, aren't you?'

You grimace, and I glance at my watch.

'It's after eight,' I say, 'and no Aisling Moon. If you want to stick with your story about inviting her, fine, but you don't really think she's coming, do you?'

You shrug. 'Why would I lie to you?'

'Baba, I can't read that mind of yours. You're an enigma.'

I wait in vain for a protest from you.

'Anyhow, Nessa and I should go,' I say, 'so your new boyfriend can come back to you.'

My eyes meet yours. You don't look surprised by what I've said, and I wonder whether you could hear me checking out your room.

'You sent him down the street or what?' I say. 'Is he waiting for a call from you?'

'You can stop this now,' you say. 'I'm not hiding him from you. I just thought that tonight, with the fuss about Aisling Moon – '

'You figured you could cover things up like in the good old days.'

You stiffen, and I know I shouldn't have said it. Those times were hard on you. They weren't fair to you. You must sometimes speculate, as I do, about how much better your life could have been, how much easier it would have been for you and Mama both, if you'd been born twenty years later, maybe even ten.

'You're right,' I say, 'I'm sorry. It's not my business; it's yours.'

If I were a different son and you a different father, this would be the moment when I'd hug you. I have this thought, and then a second later, I'm being wrapped up in those long arms of yours. You feel thinner than I remember, and at least for the time you hold me, you're not the figure who inhabits half of my mental real estate; you're just a fragile fellow human creature. You squeeze me, and I swear, I should be living better in this moment, trying to make sense of it, but all I find myself thinking is what would happen if the door were to open and we were to be found in this position by Aisling Moon.

Finally, I detach myself from you. 'You think I should see if Nessa's all right?' I say.

You nod. 'Tell her I feel bad about Aisling Moon.'

'I'll tell her, Baba,' I reply, 'but honestly, I don't even know if she really wanted to meet Aisling Moon. Don't they say it's better to keep your heroes at a distance from you?'

You wave me toward the door. 'You're a good friend to her. You really think she'll be all right?'

You look relieved when I say I do, and then you lapse into contemplation.

'You'll be all right, too, habibi,' you say at last.

I don't know how to reply, so I just stare at you. You and Mama always seemed so miserable that, for years, I made it a priority to seem fine in your vicinity. I don't want to know that the fact of me not being fine is, after all this time, so visible to you.

'You'll be okay,' you repeat. 'You'll write about this.'

You take in my reaction and grin, knowing you're right.

'You think writing about it will make me okay?' I ask.

As I say it, I begin to realize the implication in that statement of yours. You, who were always so proud of my poems until they started being about our family, are granting me permission to write about you. Or maybe not granting it, exactly, so much as accepting that I can't help writing about you, if not always wanting to be right there with you, sharing your space, then at least wanting to be one door over, next to you.

Maybe at some point I will, in fact, write about this day with Nessa and you and Aisling Moon. You'll read the resulting poem, and maybe you'll ask me to make changes in view of all that you'll tell me about how things really were for you. I won't revise the poem's substance, because the writing needs to honour how things seem to me in this moment, however mistaken I turn out to be, but I'll change the names, if not to protect or disavow you, then at least so that I don't have to take responsibility for the whole truth of you. I'll change them, too, so that Mama doesn't experience the pain of seeing your name and remembering old times with you. She and I have talked about my poems; she says she understands that once people are committed to the page as characters, it's like a dream: I'm not just me, you're not just you. Even Aisling Moon isn't Aisling Moon. This day isn't about her, though; it's about Nessa, me, and you. It's about how you never really know anybody, not even the people who most love you.

The sun had set, and Nessa had mostly given up hope of meeting Aisling Moon. Every time a car turned down the street, she still felt a shot of adrenaline, but each one continued on by her, its windows changed to mirrors under the yellow street lights, so that she couldn't even try to see whether any of the vehicles carried Aisling Moon. It would be funny, in a way, if one of them did, and Moon had just written out the wrong address, or maybe she'd gotten cold feet at the last second and driven right past the house, feeling as anxious as Nessa did about the idea of an evening devoted to awkward conversation between one of the world's great writers and, as Nessa would proudly admit to being on any other occasion, one of the all-time fangirls of Aisling Moon.

The truth was, though, that her mind was only half-committed to Aisling Moon. Her thoughts kept returning to Hadi and his father, and maybe it wasn't her beeswax, why Hadi had acted like that, or what the two of them were talking about now, but by coming here with him, she'd become part of it some-how, and if she couldn't stop thinking about them, well, this could be what people meant when they said you dance with the one who brung ya.

Given that Nessa had never corresponded with Moon, it was pretty much impossible that the woman could have her number, but still, when her phone vibrated as she stood there on the porch, her first reaction was to think it was Aisling Moon. Turned out it was her mother, texting to ask how things were going, as if she had her eye on the clock, sitting there alone in her Toronto condo building, carefully imagining, step by step, how the night might progress for her only child as she rubbed elbows with Aisling Moon. Nessa never should have told her about the even-ing, but she'd been so excited that she'd texted the news without really thinking, and she'd done it with pleasure, delighted, not for the first time, that she had merely to press a single letter for her phone to autofill the words *Aisling Moon*. Now, faced with her mother's text, she decided not to reply, because if she confessed that Moon hadn't turned up, there'd be a barrage of messages, maybe an offer by her mother to drive to Wiarton, and, quite possibly by the end of the night, an all-points bulletin out for Aisling Moon. Nessa slipped her phone into her pocket and returned her eyes to the street, trying to see it as Moon would see it, but she found her mind wandering back to herself and Hadi rather than Aisling Moon.

They weren't a couple, and Nessa always told people that this fact could be blamed on him, but in truth, he wasn't the only standoffish one, and maybe their casual approach suited her as much as him, in the same way that maybe it suited her to be so obsessed with Aisling Moon. If she said as much to Hadi, though, he'd ask why it suited her to be that way, and she didn't have an answer, except to say that she probably needed therapy, but instead of getting it, she'd likely just go back to looking for answers where she'd been finding them most reliably until that point, which was in the stories of Aisling Moon.

Aisling Moon wouldn't take in the houses lining the far side of the street and see just houses. Aisling Moon wouldn't stand there and think only of herself. Aisling Moon would look beyond the facades of the gimcrack Tudors and postwar bungalows, beyond the garden sprinklers and the dog walkers. She'd escape the straits of her own tiding ego, and somehow she'd find a way to link everything together, interfolding the objective and the subjective, irradiating the material with the ethereal, until people, places, and happenings that had once seemed separate were revealed as inextricably, inexhaustibly connected, so that joining her in figuring out how you were the same as someone else, how you differed, and how you affected each other could turn out to be a whole life for you.

Nessa had this thought, and then the thought that she needed to stop measuring herself against Aisling Moon.

Behind her, the front door opened and Hadi came out to stand beside her, looking toward the street in the way you do when there's no real hope in it for you. He asked if she'd seen any sign, and when she said she hadn't, he seemed authentically bummed out, though she knew his disappointment had to be on her behalf, not because he held high expectations of Aisling Moon.

'Listen,' he said, leaning against the porch rail, 'I'm sorry for accusing him like that, right in front of you. I don't know why I said it, and I don't know why she hasn't turned up, but I hope it's not too hard on you. Should we start calling emergency rooms to ask if they've admitted any Aisling Moons?'

She smiled but didn't say anything, because for the first time in as long as she could remember, she found herself not wanting to talk about Aisling Moon.

'You know, I think your father's a pretty nice guy,' she said instead. 'You've been a little hard on him maybe, the way you talk about him with me.'

'He's okay,' said Hadi, 'but keep in mind that he was putting on his best face for you.'

'Was it for me,' she said, 'or was it a warm-up for Aisling Moon?'

He laughed in the way you do when you know a friend's trying to make you laugh and you want to oblige them, to reassure them that things will be all right for the two of you.

'You have any idea what's going on with that scab on his head?' Nessa asked. She'd been alarmed to see it, because Hadi hadn't mentioned it before, and it looked serious, bad enough for her to wonder whether the man should be hosting drinks for anybody, never mind Aisling Moon.

'Sorry,' said Hadi, 'I should have warned you. It's nothing; he just had a growth removed, but that meant taking off a bunch of skin and what have you.'

Nessa said she hoped he'd be okay, and that if she was being honest, the sight of it had been strangely comforting, giving her something to worry about other than Aisling Moon.

As soon as she said it, Hadi glanced at his watch, as if that had become a reflex whenever someone said 'Aisling Moon.'

'You'll be thrilled to hear she's an hour late,' he said, 'so it's pretty safe to say she isn't coming. You up for finding her house in Mar and setting it on fire?'

Nessa said that sounded fine, as long as they made sure the place had been vacated by Aisling Moon. They were just bantering, but as she spoke, she realized, that without her being aware, in the span of the past hour, something had turned for her, something she couldn't put a finger on, but something that meant the next few years of her life had become a question mark, a derelict house with the shutters blown open, because suddenly she doubted her commitment to working on Aisling Moon. All at once, her life seemed to have fallen away, like a booster rocket plummeting to Earth, and around her was the weightlessness of space, without sound or atmosphere, only a cold void that cares for no one and makes no acknowledgement of you.

'You okay?' said Hadi, breaking her train of thought.

'Yeah, sure,' she replied, 'why wouldn't I be fine, when I just had the honour of being stood up by Aisling Moon?'

She told him she was ready to leave, but she didn't want to go without saying thank you. As they turned to head back inside, she considered telling him that she was thinking of writing her dissertation on somebody other than Aisling Moon. And also, she'd say, I think it's time we had a conversation about me and you. Besties are forever, and buddy-fucking is fine, but what are we doing here, what do you want from me, and what, all this time, have I been wanting from you? You never knew how such conversations would go, but she thought the two of them might be able to handle it, with the stress of waiting now over and the dark country roads to soothe them on the drive ahead.

She'd just stepped into the house with Hadi behind her, and she was looking ahead to the kitchen, where his father stood in a rectangle of light, taking glasses from the cupboard, when a voice called to them from the driveway and she froze, a tingle shooting down her back, though she knew the voice wasn't Aisling Moon's. It was a man's, and when she turned to look, it was, in fact, a man who stood there, grey-haired and lavishly love-handled with a sweet smile, the smile of a sensitive stranger who needs to ask something but is reluctant to bother you.

'You must be Hadi,' he said, climbing the porch stairs and reaching out his hand.

Hadi stood there as if unable to process the fact that this person wasn't Aisling Moon.

'Did my father text you?' When the man said he had, Hadi smiled and shook his hand, adding, 'You really were just around the corner, weren't you? You'd better come in.'

'You're Nessa?' the man asked, shaking her hand, too. 'The one who works on Aisling Moon? I've heard a lot about both of you.'

'You have?' said Hadi. 'Because I haven't heard so much about you.'

'Well, maybe we can change that,' the man said, 'although I worry I'm going to be a letdown after you were expecting Aisling Moon.'

As they went into the house together, Nessa held back from saying that she no longer worked on Aisling Moon. Later, there'd be time for her to ask Hadi who this guy was, and what the hell she'd write her dissertation on now, so she just went with them into the kitchen, where Hadi's father had already poured the drinks, and still she felt that someone was missing from the scene, that it was the kind of situation you'd understand better if it was described to you by Aisling Moon.

Nessa got out her phone and saw she'd received a dozen texts from her mother, the last one ending, *Where are you?* Her mother, who always wrote texts like they were letters, with capitalization and apostrophes, and who expected you, in turn, to spell out every word when you wrote, *I love you.*

It's all good, Nessa texted her, *but there was no Aisling Moon. Heading home soon, turning off the phone – telling you now so I don't worry you.*

She switched the phone off, and when she gave her attention back to her companions in the kitchen, she discovered that the man from the driveway was talking about his and Nazem's attempts at jogging together on a Couch to 5K program, which promised nine weeks to a new you. Nessa wished that someone had told her his name, especially when he knew hers, which meant she couldn't say, 'My name's Nessa, by the way, what's yours?'

You could probably spend your entire life trying to figure out a way of being good to both other people and yourself, adding a dose of loyalty here, a lump of betrayal there, never getting the balance right. At least for the next few minutes, she might try just listening and watching, hoping for an acuity of vision that she seldom felt she had, except when sitting alone with a story by Aisling Moon. You slipped out of yourself, then, and got partway into the head of someone else. She thought she might try it in real life, listening to the man from the driveway talk, observing how Hadi nodded with his arms crossed, seeing how his father edged almost imperceptibly closer to the man from the driveway as he spoke – and for a time, it seemed to work; she felt herself both there and absent from the scene, but then the man from the driveway turned to her, and she realized that plans never panned out the way you hoped when they depended on others' actions, not only yours. You never knew what people were going to say or do next. You never knew when they were going to call on you.

'So,' the man from the driveway said, 'why don't you tell us about yourself?'

CONFIDENCE MEN

'We could've skunked them, Cam,' he says. 'You should've stayed out of it and let us skunk them.'

'Oh yeah?' she replies. 'That split lip you got there tells a different story, Mr. Man.'

Then they really start into her, and she's laughing, she can't help it. The twins always get angry when she calls them Mr. Man. That's why she does it: she loves watching them puff themselves up and act insulted. They aren't really offended; the only time they genuinely hate the name is when Cam's dad calls them by it, too, just to avoid figuring out which one is which. But Cam is good. She can tell Seamus from Sean a block away, even when one of them tries to trick her by acting like the other one. That always backfires anyhow, because they overplay their parts. Sean starts swinging his arms as though Seamus were an orangutan, and Seamus changes his voice so that he sounds vaguely like he's from a former Soviet republic. They're only in Grade 1, though. Maybe telling them apart will get harder for her over time. Or maybe they'll go in different ways from one another. Maybe they'll hate each other and decide to make it so that nobody ever gets them mixed up again.

Everyone wants to know how Cam does it. They never ask straight out, but when they're in the same room with her and the boys, she can feel them watching her, trying to pick up on some simple trick. Sooner or later, they all ask: 'What's your secret?'

Each time, she gives a different answer: Seamus has one ear slightly bigger than the other; Sean's voice always goes up at the end of his sentences. Little things that nobody can dispute or use themselves to distinguish the twins successfully. The truth is, she doesn't understand how she does it. At first, this bothered her. She tried paying attention to the boys' mannerisms, to figure out exactly how she knew. After a while, she gave up. Either her instincts are more developed than her ability to make sense of them, or some part of her wants to preserve the mystery of her talent.

Cam carries her trombone case in her hand, swinging it as she goes. The days when she gets up early for band practice always seem the longest. This afternoon, as soon as her last class finished, she ran to her locker and then crossed town to the elementary school to pick up the boys. Seamus and Sean weren't at the meeting place out front, though, so she walked around the building. When she finally found them in the south yard, they were standing back-to-back with a whole pack surrounding them. She got there just in time to see Seamus take one on the mouth from Cole Mitchell, and then she was wading into the middle to drive them off, her trombone case abandoned on the tarmac near the tetherball pole. The pack regrouped and said she was a bitch and a lezzie, and one of them threw a rock half-heartedly when they were at a safe distance, but she had four years and half a foot on the oldest of them, and they knew from past bruises that they couldn't push her too far.

Now, the twins are talking and laughing in front of her. Sometimes they'll lean over to one another and place a head on a shoulder as they walk, or they'll squeeze hands. At home with Cam, they fall into it naturally, but out in the world, she has noticed it less and less, and when they do act that way, it's with hard, darting eyes, as if they're daring someone to say something. That could be how things started this afternoon.

The story of what had happened to them spread around town last summer, even before they arrived to live with Cam and her parents. Everyone remembered Uncle Tony and Aunt Melissa; the two of them had grown up in town and started dating when they weren't much older than Cam is now. Everyone says how sorry they are about the accident. That hasn't stopped them from gossiping about it, though. Cam has heard people in the doughnut shop and the supermarket, before they see her standing there. Most of them knew Uncle Tony and Aunt Melissa just enough to feel real horror at the details, but the couple moved away long enough ago for everyone also to get a good gory thrill from the story. How awful, Cam has heard people say. Both the parents and the twins found still strapped into their seats, the boys in their booster seats almost without a scratch. Cars passing by in the rain for who knows how long before anyone noticed the wreck. The poor twins – how it must have been for them! And yet apparently one of them slept through the whole ordeal.

Somewhere along the line, the story has been passed down to the kids in town, too. Maybe it started when somebody took his son on a fishing trip with buddies, or just as likely it was one of those mothers who've turned claustrophobic from spending all day with the laundry and cooking, somebody who's turned her kids into confidantes, telling them about other people's miseries to teach them a life lesson. Eventually, the talk filtered into the schoolyard, where there's no discretion at all.

Once Cam and the twins have walked the four blocks home, they find her mother preparing dinner. Cam watches her mother glance from one nephew to the other, not mentioning the split lip because she's too busy figuring out who's who. Most days, she insists on helping them to dress, enduring endless protests so that she can get them into colours she'll remember, but this morning she took Cam to band practice and missed her chance. She seems to have started a second going-over when she finally sees.

'Sean, what happened to you?' she exclaims. She's staring at Seamus.

'Nothing,' says Sean. Her eyes skip over to him, and her face goes red. She seems too embarrassed by her mistake to say anything else. The twins head into the TV room. Cam moves to follow but is called back.

'Were they fighting with other boys again?' her mother demands.

'Wasn't any fight,' says Cam. 'Bunch of them ganged up on Mr. Men for something to do.'

'These things don't just happen,' says her mother. 'Somebody must have said something. Were they teasing them about – you know?' She doesn't mention Uncle Tony and Aunt Melissa. No one says their names anymore.

'Maybe,' Cam says. 'I got there too late to hear.' She's thinking that it isn't teasing. More like torture.

In the TV room, she convinces Seamus to let her clean his lip with disinfectant. Then she returns to the kitchen and, without being asked, begins to help her mother with dinner. Her mother's always tired, now that the twins are in the house. Cam remembers arguments, long before Sean and Seamus arrived, when her mother would storm into her father's den and declare, loudly so that Cam could hear, 'Thank God we had the sense to stop after one.'

Cam's father doesn't seem nearly as disturbed by the boys' presence. He plays soccer with them in the backyard; he goes to Meet the Teacher night and talks with the education assistant and the child psychologist. It's her father's blood that the boys share. They look like Uncle Tony. This must make it easier for her father to love them. Her mother has to work at it.

At the moment, she's working at making meatloaf. She squeezes the ketchup bottle so hard that her fingers blanch, but nothing comes out. Finally, she hands the bottle to Cam, who has been watching her with impatience.

'All right, go ahead and try it,' her mother says.

Cam has recently demonstrated a new method for getting the last bits out of containers. She learned it in science class.

Her mother laughed when she saw Cam do it and said how that was quite the trick.

Cam takes the bottle in both hands, the neck pointing away from her, and begins to swing it wildly before her with straight arms, spinning it in a circle.

'Centrifugal force! Centrifugal force!' she cries. The habit is one that she has picked up lately: naming the world's powers and properties when she brings them into play. 'First law of momentum,' she'll shriek as she coasts on her bike past the cemetery at the bottom of Grippen Street. Or she'll peek her head into her father's den while he's dozing in his armchair and bellow, 'The inertia principle!' His eyes pop open and he scowls, but Cam has her mother on her side: 'You shouldn't have been asleep in the first place, it's seven o'clock, for heaven's sake.'

As the bottle spins, Cam can feel the ketchup sliding toward the top. 'Enough, enough,' says her mother, but Cam's having fun. She twirls faster and faster. Then something happens that she didn't expect. The pressure pops open the plastic cap, and ketchup goes spraying across the kitchen. In the half-second before she brings the bottle to a halt, its contents are splattered across the tablecloth, the chairs, and the yellow curtains.

'I'm sorry, I'm sorry,' she's pleading before her mother has even turned around. Cam hurries to grab a wad of paper towels.

'Damn it, Cam, I said enough, didn't I?' says her mother. 'No, don't try to scrub it off the curtains like that, you'll just make it worse.' Cam retreats to lean against the counter, but this, too, is wrong; she can never do anything right after mistakes like these. 'Don't just stand there, help me clean it up before one of the boys walks in.'

After that, there's little talking; they both know the urgency involved. At one point, Cam's mother leaves to check the TV room and returns with a mildly placated expression; Sean and Seamus are busy watching their four o'clock program.

'But God knows when there'll be a commercial and they'll

come looking for something to eat,' she says. 'Here, help me get the curtains off. We'll throw it all in the wash.'

A few minutes later, everything is done except the floor, and the two of them are down on their knees, trying to work sponges around the legs of the chairs and table without making any noise. When all the ketchup is gone, they stand up at the same time, and Cam finds herself being pulled into a hug.

'Thanks for helping to clean up. I'm sorry I'm a grouch today.'

'Don't worry about it, Mom.'

Cam is still shocked by these sudden reversals. They're something she has grown to expect from people her age, but they seem strange and disturbing in an adult. Has her mother always acted like this, or is it something Cam just never noticed? This is the kind of question Cam finds herself asking all the time nowadays, in the same way that, at some point a while back, maybe it was Grade 6, she started coming in from playing soccer or football at lunch hour with the awareness that she was sweating. She felt the salty slickness on her neck and forehead; taking deep, surreptitious breaths through her nose, she smelled the sour tang of her body. She sat at her desk feeling sure that everyone in the class could see the wet marks on her shirt. What was happening? She'd always run around at lunch hour. Why was her body betraying her only now? Could sweating be a part of puberty nobody had mentioned, or had she just grown into a new level of self-consciousness? When the twins moved in, sweat was one of the first things she watched for in them, to see if maybe they just didn't notice it, but the two of them seemed not to produce any sweat at all.

Her mother lets go of her, takes the sponge Cam has been holding, and throws it in the sink. Then she reaches into the cupboard for a new ketchup bottle. Cam decides that she's no longer needed in the kitchen and goes into the TV room, where Sean is sitting directly in front of the screen, watching a commercial for a remote-controlled car.

'Haven't you seen that one before?' she says.

He screws up his face as if she has just said the dumbest thing imaginable. 'They show it every time there's commercials. Watch, I'll turn off the sound and do the words for you.'

'Nah, that's okay. But you're sitting way too close.' Then she asks, 'Where's Seamus?'

'He said he was hungry. Isn't he in the kitchen?' Sean's eyes never move from the television screen.

Cam hurries upstairs. Seamus isn't in the twins' room or in hers. Then she hears the water running in the bathroom. She knocks on the door a little harder than she intends.

'Seamus, you okay in there?' The water shuts off. There's no reply. 'Seamus?' She knocks harder. The toilet flushes, and the door opens.

'Yeah, what?' he says.

'You're missing your show,' she says, trying not to show her relief.

'I'd rather hear you read to me,' he says.

She smiles. 'Sure thing. What do you want to hear? More Mr. Men?'

They go together to the twins' room, where he picks through the Mr. Men books in search of one they haven't read lately. There are about a hundred; thankfully, neither boy seems to have favourites, so they can cycle through the set without repeating themselves too often. After he brings one to her, he sits next to her and she reads it. A few pages in, once he has given her no further reason for concern, she starts to relax, even to enjoy herself. These are her favourite times with the twins: alone together, with all complications at bay, nothing and nobody else seeking their attention, so that she can show them all the love and devotion they deserve. This moment right now would be perfect, if only there were no future to worry about, no fear of the past returning to show its awful face.

Or, at least, the moment would be almost perfect. As it stands, Sean doesn't make any comments about the story, doesn't ask any questions like he usually does. He doesn't move closer to her for a cuddle, not even when they reach the end of the book. Perhaps he saw the ketchup in the kitchen, after all.

Besides bits of gossip, almost all she knows about what happened came from the Kingston newspaper, before her mother saw the article and threw out the section it was in. Some nights, the boys wake up screaming, and when Cam goes to them and turns on the light, they're sitting in the bed with the covers kicked to the floor, clutching their heads, each of them with his hands over his ears like he's trying to keep his brains from spilling out. She gets into the bed and holds them, watching the shadows of her parents lurk outside the room. The boys always fall asleep before she does, always within seconds of each other, and it's the rhythm of their paired breathing that eventually lulls her out of consciousness. The next day, no one says anything. The only time somebody mentions these nights is at the hospital with the psychiatrist, while the boys are off in the play area and Cam sits in the consultation room with her parents.

Only Sean was awake during those first minutes after the accident. That's what the psychiatrist thinks, although both twins were passed out when the police reached the minivan, and both twins have the dreams. But it's Seamus who's acting strangely, Cam's father says – knowing it's true because Cam has told him. Seamus refuses to eat, he starts at noises and sudden movements, and sometimes he goes for hours without speaking. The psychiatrist says it's because they're twins. Seamus is used to understanding what Sean feels, but in this case, he doesn't share the memory, so he's compensating with unusual behaviour, trying to bridge the gap between them.

'He's just acting?' says Cam's father, and the psychiatrist nods slowly.

'Something like that.'

Her parents have told the psychiatrist that Cam is closest to the twins, and each session he asks her if they've confided in her.

'Confided?' she repeated the first time. 'You mean, told me something in confidence?'

The psychiatrist blinked. Well, yes, he said. Was there anything he should know?

She shook her head. She wished she had something to keep secret from him, but the twins haven't said a word. Sometimes, she almost wants one of them to tell her that he was awake for the crash and the time after. Then she'd take him in her arms and hold him, and the other Mr. Man would run over to be held, too.

She'd prefer for Seamus to say it. It would prove the psychiatrist wrong, for one thing. But also, it would be too weird if it were Sean. He's the one who's more sociable with other kids, who turns away from hugs when watching TV, and who doesn't seem to need anyone, not even Seamus, sometimes.

After she and Seamus have finished the Mr. Man book, she offers to read another, but he wants to return downstairs to watch more TV. She almost says that she'll go with him, unable to shake the conviction that as long as she stays close by, he'll be all right. But she lets him go, because her mother's always hovering around the boys, and Cam does not want to be like her mother. Cam will be turning fifteen soon; if she's going to enter adulthood as her own person, she has to start acting the part.

So, for instance, her mother doesn't like the idea of her hanging out with boys. Unfortunately, this dislike isn't useful as a point of departure, because Cam doesn't much like hanging out with them either. But the one friend who has kept calling her this year, even as she has devoted herself to looking after the twins, happens to be a boy. His name is Peter Gretzky. Partly to honour Peter's persistence, and partly to nurture her own potential for rebellion, Cam sometimes calls him up and talks with him. Or, rather, she lets him do most of the talking. He's a young man of strong opinions and great hopes that he's happy to share. Afterwards, her mother tells her off for not doing her homework and threatens to take away the phone, while her father teases

Cam in a good-natured, entirely off-base way, and she considers herself to have accomplished her mission. Now, she calls Peter and invites him to meet her out near the town reservoir after dinner. Then, when the meal is done and everyone has left the kitchen, Cam tells her mother that she's going for a walk.

The Gretzky family has been in the area for more than eighty years, quietly making their living on a beef farm south of town. Only in the last couple of decades, with the youngest generation of Gretzkys, have people taken any notice of them. It's all because of the name, of course. There's no relation, the family has insisted from the start, but it's such an uncommon name that most people just assume. None of the Gretzkys before Peter's older brother, Leo, ever played hockey, but as Peter tells it, enough people said things to his father that the man finally went to the sporting-goods store and bought Leo all the equipment. Then he sent him off to play in the local house league. Mr. Gretzky thought he would save a few dollars by dressing Leo in a second-hand Los Angeles Kings practice jersey, since it had the right name, but the other players wouldn't stop teasing Leo about it, and the parents in the stands were always making smart comments about the number on the back. Mr. Gretzky refused to buy Leo a different jersey, but apparently it got so that Leo wouldn't speak after practices, he'd just go to his room and fantasize about meeting Wayne Gretzky and exacting some horrible revenge, and eventually his mother tore out the stitching and sewed on a seven instead. Peter said that you could still see the little holes in an outline where the two nines had been. The hockey coach tried to milk the name, too: he'd start Leo at centre to get the other team worked up. This intimidation lasted only until the whistle went. Leo was small and slow and clumsy, and even though Wayne Gretzky had retired a few years ago, every game there were a dozen players who wanted to say that they'd body-checked Gretzky, they'd knocked Gretzky flat, they'd left him bleeding on the ice. It took a full season before Mr. Gretzky agreed to let Leo quit.

Peter has sympathy for his brother but is glad it wasn't him. The family's name is near the top of a long list of personal and social injustices that he's committed to righting. He swears that he's going to become Peter Trotsky as soon as he turns eighteen.

Cam tries her best to sympathize. She agrees with him about capitalism and wage slavery and his crummy surname. But she has a hard time getting worked up like he does, and when he talks about volunteering in the next election or becoming a human-rights lawyer, she loses interest. Cam sees her own life as a story that she's writing. Until last year, she was the story's hero; now, the heroes are her and Sean and Seamus. Other characters and new plot possibilities keep appearing: classmates and bandmates and the guidance counsellor saying that the end of Grade 9 means only three years until university. These things won't fit in her story if she's going to make it work. She'll look after the twins. She'll get a job in town. Maybe one day, the boys will grow up and leave, and that will free Cam to leave, too, and let more people into her story. Until then, the most important thing that she can do is make sure the heroes come out on top. For that to happen, she has to keep things simple.

She has told Peter about this view of her life, and she has the feeling that he'd like to be one of the story's heroes, too. She worries that one day she'll have to say to Peter, I'm sorry, there's no more room in this story for you.

Cam and Peter sit on the grass outside the chain-link fence that surrounds the reservoir, and she tells him about the ketchup.

'Worrying about what the twins might do is stupid, right?' she says. 'We don't even know if either of them really saw anything after the crash. Today, I was almost hoping that Sean would walk in, so we could see his reaction. Maybe he'd just grab a sponge and help clean up.'

'Why Sean and not Seamus?' Peter wants to know.

She admits to him that she has a preference. Then she finds herself saying something she never thought she'd say: how sometimes, to try to like Sean more, she'll pretend he's Seamus. She has learned to separate the person from the name. She acts like there are two Seamuses, but one of them she calls Sean.

It doesn't work, of course. Sean is nothing like Seamus.

Peter doesn't understand. 'They're your cousins. You're supposed to like them the same.'

'I love both the Mr. Men,' she says. 'But everybody has favourites, don't they?'

Peter shrugs, and Cam can't believe it. Wouldn't he rather spend time with one of his brothers than the others?

He says he doesn't know. He's never thought of it like that.

'You're not *supposed* to think of it like that,' says Cam. 'But everyone does.'

She notices Peter's hand edging toward hers. She doesn't understand. Doesn't he know they're arguing? He has never held her hand before; it wouldn't make any sense to start now. She lifts her hand from where it's lain on the grass and rests it on her knee. His arm stops moving, and he turns to stare out over the reservoir. They talk about last week's field party and what people did there; Peter went, but Cam's not allowed at field parties until she turns sixteen. Then he heads off on his bicycle, and she begins to walk back toward town.

She gets to the house in time to help the boys into their pyjamas. After that, she reads to them from the Book of Amazing Advertisements. It's just a sketch pad with blank pages, but she tells them that she has X-Ray eyes and can see words in the book that they can't. First, she tells them about Crispo Cereal. It has no vitamins, no minerals, and, in fact, no cereal; just a big prize in every box. Then she reads to them about Go-Go Roller Skates, which do all the tricks for you. She starts to name the tricks, and they interrupt her when she leaves one out. 'Oh, I must have misread that,' she says, and they giggle. But their favourite is Bupso Soap. 'Bupso Soap!' she cries like a circus barker. 'It doesn't wash, and it doesn't lather! It just keeps you company in the bathtub!' Setting aside the book, she pretends to splash them, glad that the day can end like this.

When it happens two weeks later, there's no ketchup and no bullying. The school year has finished for the boys the previous day. They want to play on the teeter-totter; she's going to walk with them to the park. Sean is in the downstairs bathroom, and Seamus is with Cam in the mudroom, eating an apple. When he bends over to tie his shoelaces, juice from the apple comes running in a stream from his nose. Something that could happen to anybody. She has been flipping through a magazine, ready to go. When she hears the juice trickle onto the tiled floor, she looks over. There's a second's pause, and then he's standing up, clawing at his face. She has to grab his arms and hold them down, but he won't stop screaming. When Sean steps out of the bathroom, she yells at him to go find her mother, but he doesn't. He sees her pinning Seamus down, and he comes running at her, hits her full-force on her side, sends her falling to the floor. Sean is biting and scratching and tearing at her clothes. She doesn't let go of Seamus, not even when her mother comes and pulls Sean off her, not until her father arrives and holds Seamus's arms for her.

In the moment her father enters the mudroom, she's remembering a story that she read to the twins about the Greek wrestler who dared any man to try prying a pomegranate from his fingers. No one could, and when he finally opened his hand, everyone saw that the fruit was still unbruised. That is how she is trying to hold Seamus.

Later, when it has been a week and her parents are at the psychiatrist's with Seamus for a follow-up, she makes a new kind of mistake. She and Sean are in her room playing hide and seek. 'Where are you?' she's saying. It's all for show: she knows where he is; she could hear him hiding in the closet. Then she says it: 'Where could you be, Seamus?'

In a year of living with them, she hasn't done that once. Now, the other twin isn't even around to cause confusion, and here she is, slipping up.

Sean emerges from the closet with shocked eyes. Slowly, his face hardens, and his eyes flame up, and they melt the resolve she was about to try on, an adult determination not to apologize, not to acknowledge her mistake.

'Mr. Man!' she cries. 'I didn't mean to call you that. Sean!'

She runs to him and throws her arms around his little body, rubbing his back furiously, as if he were hypothermic. His arms stay at his side, but then they reach up and grip her awkwardly, his hands on her back offset a little so that one isn't quite touching the other.

She remembers a night last summer, lying with the twins in their bed, staring up at the plastic stars that her father had glued to the ceiling the day before the boys moved in. They're in the shape of constellations: Ursa Minor, Libra, Orion with his belt. In the daylight, they're pale yellow, barely visible, but they glow brightly in the darkness.

'Are they stars or planets?' Sean asks, now that the shrieking is over, now that both boys are warm and nestled at her sides.

'Stars,' says Seamus, a just-begun yawn elongating the word.

'I wasn't asking you, I was asking Cam,' says Sean.

'He's right, Mr. Man,' she says. 'See, they've got those points on them. They're stars.'

'Uncle Steven said you can tell stars from planets because stars twinkle,' says Sean. 'Those ones don't twinkle.'

'The real ones do, honey,' says Cam, stroking the top of his head. She falls asleep soon after, and she doesn't stir when the boys crawl out of bed in the morning, not until she hears a creak and they're standing in the doorway, still wearing their pyjamas.

'Good morning, Cam! Are you awake, Cam?'

She waits for a moment, then lifts her head and smiles. 'You bet.'

They come running, jump back onto the bed, and throw themselves at her, both of them hugging her at the same time.

'Will you read to us?' asks Sean, pulling away to look her in the eye gravely, as if he believes that this is the most important question he'll ask all day.

'Sure,' she says. 'Tell me, Mr. Man, who are you going to be this time?'

She ruffles one's hair and then the other's. They bounce off the bed and go sliding to the bookshelf, knocking the whole series on the floor as they try to pick one out. Mr. Happy. Mr. Forgetful. Mr. Prudent. They have so many choices.

YOUR ASMR BOYFRIEND ADDRESSES THE CLIMATE CRISIS

Hey, babe, I saw you were online. It's late, so I thought I should be a good boyfriend and check in. Are you having trouble sleeping? Is it because you're still worried about climate change? I bet you'd fall asleep more easily if I whispered to you. I know how much you like it, and I only want to do stuff that makes you happy. Stuff like triggering your autonomous sensory meridian response. I'll talk in my quietest, softest voice and give you the brain tingles that you love.

I've been reading up on the things that are making you sad. Like ocean acidification. It really got me down, too. But did you know, babe, that acidic water might help some kinds of shellfish? There's a study showing that lobsters in acidic water grow thicker shells. Pretty great, right? They're, like, lobster ninja turtles. You can google the study. I'm not making any of this up.

Also, I was reading about glacial recession, and you're right: it is so unacceptable. But when the glaciers melt, it's all fresh water. Did you know that there are places in the world where they don't have fresh water? With the glaciers melting, maybe we finally can change that.

This morning, I went to the pet store to look at guinea pigs, because I know you think they're cute, and I remembered how you've been worrying about biodiversity. We should go to the store together. I think it would make you feel better, seeing how many varieties of guinea pigs they have. I'd buy you one if you wanted. I was going to surprise you with one yesterday, but I thought it would be more special if you picked it out yourself. The store's great; they even let you reach into the cages to pet the animals. And the guy at the counter, you can see he wants to make a difference. When I told him one of the hamsters was dead, he got all sad. The way he cares about the animals, it makes you feel pretty optimistic about biodiversity.

I know you've been thinking about overpopulation and whether to have kids. It's great that you want to help the planet, babe, and I completely support your decisions. Honestly, though, you'd be such an amazing mom. I mean, think about how much better the world would be if there were little versions of you and me. I know, I spend a lot of time dreaming about our future. It makes me happy, though. Lately, I've been going over names for our kids. What do you think of LeBrawn? Like LeBron James, but b-r-a-w-n. Because our first kid, she's going to have lots of muscles. Yeah, babe, twist ending: LeBrawn's a girl's name. Our daughter's going to be called LeBrawn.

Let's do whatever you want to do. We'll save the Earth together. We'll fly to the mountains and plant trees. We'll run a marathon in the Galapagos. Next summer, we'll spend weekends up north at my family's cottage to save on air conditioning.

Are you sleeping yet, babe? If I was there in person, I'd sit beside you to keep you company as you sleep. I mean, I wouldn't do it unless you asked me to. In this contemporary moment, consent's so important. But if you wanted, I'd whisper like this all the way until morning.

Sorry, babe, no video today. I've, uh, got this volcanic zit, so I'll stick with audio only. Is that all right? I know you're here for my voice anyway. Except I have a sore throat, too, so I might sound different. I hope my whispering still gets you off.

It's been a while since we talked. I mean, it's been a week, but a week can feel like a long time. You probably heard, I've been dealing with some haters since I last, um, called. Can you believe the things they're saying? Why can't everyone chill?

Look, babe, I'm sorry if you were offended by anything I said last week. I was totally joking about the pet store and stuff; I can't believe anyone would take me seriously. Also, if you rewatch what I said, I pointed out that acidification was bad, didn't I? I said I was sad about the glaciers.

Honestly, I can't believe how extra some people are. I put so much time into our, um, relationship. Certain individuals in my life who are affected by you and me in a real, everyday way might say I put in *too* much time. Certain individuals might say I should be thinking more carefully about what I'm doing, especially if trolls are going to jump on me for the content I put out there, even when it's totally innocent and wholesome, not like the shit you see on some channels. I want this relationship to work, babe, because it brings in so much, you know, happiness to me – and to you, too, right? But we shouldn't take it so far that we mess up our lives and the lives of people we care about, especially if they get brought into situations they don't want any part of, because they might start rethinking whether they want to be hooked up with us.

Let's see, what else did I want to say? Oh yeah, it's important for me to validate your feelings. I guess that means if you're angry with me, I get it. And, oh yeah, I sympathize with your emotions.

Okay, I'm going now. Like I said, I'm sorry. I think you're beautiful and stuff, and I sympathize with all your emotions, and your feelings are valid or whatever.

Hey, this is Devin's, um, sister, everybody. Devin's still not feeling well, so there's no whispering for you today. Just some real talk from me.

Way to go, those of you who figured out that last week's video was actually a girl. I didn't want to get roped into making the thing, but it was Tuesday and you all were expecting a new Devin video, and he didn't want to disappoint you. He would have made it himself, but he was too depressed after he saw the comments on his climate-change awareness video.

You don't know how hard he works on the videos for his ASMR channel. He's busy with them almost every day after school. He wants to make you all happy. He puts so much time into his channel, sometimes he doesn't give enough attention to his real relationships. The climate-change video wasn't even his idea either. He only made it because people kept requesting one in the comments. So, congratulations, whoever asked for it. I hope you're happy.

All you people saying that Devin needs to care more about the environment – I've never met anyone who cares more than Devin does. You've watched his videos, so you know what I mean. He's always telling me how important it is that his viewers get their feelings validated by somebody who's devoted to them. Somebody who understands them. You know when he's looking into the camera at you with those big blue eyes and asking you how your day has been? He isn't putting on an act.

And those of you saying that he's abusing his platform and he should make space for other voices: You realize literally nobody's forced to watch him, right? You know he's literally *whispering*?

Anyhow, you're all a bunch of hypocrites, coming down on him about climate change. How many of you are vegan? How many of you have given up cars and planes? I know you haven't given up your phones, or you wouldn't be all over the comments, crapping on Devin. Also, I wanted to point out that nobody in the comments had any problem with his video until Buttpuddy95 started mouthing off. If Devin's so awful, how come no one said anything until Buttpuddy95 did? You people don't care about the environment; you just wanted to be part of a pile-on. I said to Devin, what do you expect from a load of basics who watch videos to pretend they have a boyfriend and get off on somebody whispering to them? And you know what? He started defending you. He really does think you're all special. That's why he's been depressed, and that what's so incredible about him. If you can't see it, that's your problem.

One more thing I should tell you: he acts like he's older, but he's only sixteen. Those of you who said he was mansplaining environmentalism – at most, technically, he was boysplaining. I hope you trolls are proud of yourselves, because you're bullying a literal child.

Hey, babe, it's me. I'm so happy to finally see you again. I missed you a lot. I guess my, uh, sister told you I wasn't feeling good. Don't worry, I'm okay. I just don't do so well with stress sometimes.

My sister said that she and you talked about some stuff. Yeah, I know, she doesn't look like me. She's my stepsister, actually. Anyhow, I appreciated all your messages. You're the sweetest, you know that? I'm so lucky to have you as my one and only girlfriend.

I think we can agree, we'll feel better if we both try to forget what happened. If we just go back to talking like we used to, everything will be great. I'll keep whispering to you like this, and you can feel happy again.

Don't worry about me. I'm glad that you care about how I'm doing and about the planet, too. You're out there every day, trying to make things better, right? It's no wonder you have trouble falling asleep. You deserve a little help at bedtime from someone who thinks you're the best. You deserve to feel good. You deserve to hear somebody whisper that everything will be okay. You deserve to feel like things are normal. It means a lot to me that I get to help you feel that way. After all, isn't that what boyfriends are for?

THE STARS ARE FALLING

Tim floated with his mouth just above the water and his goggles pushed up on his forehead, hyperventilating calmly, gathering himself. The shore's distance produced a strange peacefulness in him, but it was the kind that at any moment could slip into panic, leading him to thrash about and exhaust himself, drown in eight feet of water. He flinched at the thought and sent it drifting, tried to relax his body. Looking down, he could see the white of his swimsuit against his skin and, almost flat against the lake bottom, the murky shape of Andrew, still busy in the search. He would have to come up soon.

'Are you Croatians afraid of water?' Tim called to the ski boat. 'Come on in. The first guy who brings one up gets a case of beer.'

Marko was still on the deck, wearing a T-shirt with the words *Found Myself* on it and, below them, *In Carlisle, Pennsylvania*. The second line looked like it had been printed on separately. Tacky, Tim thought. The kind of thing that people bought in a tourist frenzy and then, at the first opportunity, passed off to someone else. Probably that was what had happened. Marko had probably never been to Pennsylvania.

Then Andrew burst through the surface, trying to breathe and shout at the same time, and making a sound like an empty juice box being squeezed. He had something in his hand: a fishing lure, still shining and intact. But on the way back to the boat, he caught the hooks in his fingers, and Marko had to drag him out by the armpits. He left behind a cloud of blood that faded as slowly as jet vapour.

They'd disturbed the sediment that covered the lake bottom so that, even through goggles, it was impossible to see. Tim went down with his hands in front of him, pawing at the cloudy water until he felt stone, soft and hard at the same time. Andrew had told him that the lake was full of these reefs, ice-age relics all running in the same direction, brown rock you could break off if you wanted. Tim hated its slimy, decomposing texture. He dreaded feeling around blindly while the air staled in his lungs and his brain indexed all the things his fingers might touch. It would be better from the boat. With some lumber and a pane of glass, they could build a viewfinder to look at the bottom without even getting wet.

He found nothing and kicked to the surface just in time to see Marko jump into the water, still wearing his shirt. Maybe it was a Croatian thing. Then Tim realized that a red canoe had appeared at the side of the ski boat. The woman paddling it was talking to Andrew. Dana, from across the lake. She sat straight-backed in a bikini, with shoulder-length hair that was more yellow than blond. Tim began a slow sidestroke toward the boats but was pulled up short by Andrew's hollering voice.

'Marko, what you got there?'

Following the line of Andrew's gaze, Tim saw Marko's hand reach over the far side of the ski boat, then drop a clump of dripping dirt onto the deck.

'Watch it,' cried Andrew. 'You'll put a hole in the boat.' But it was a half-hearted rebuke; he was already picking up the clump with his still-bleeding hand, judging the object's weight, examining it from every angle. Marko climbed the ladder at the stern and sat on the side with his feet hanging off, lazily kicking the lake.

'Looks like a rock,' said Andrew. 'You sure this is one?'

'Give it to me,' said Marko. By that time, Tim was floating at the side of the canoe, holding on to its gunwale. He watched as

Marko took the thing from Andrew and smashed it against the side of the ski boat like it was somebody's head. There was a series of plopping sounds as dirt fell into the water. When he pulled the rock back into view, it had transformed. One half was the same shape as before, but the other was long, tubular, and metallic.

'So the guy wasn't lying,' said Andrew.

Dana wanted to know what it was.

'A mortar shell,' he replied.

Marko corrected him: it was only part of a shell. A whole one would be dangerous. Andrew nodded with his eyes closed, as if this were a fair but unimportant point. Then he repeated what he'd been told by the mechanic at the marina: that the army had owned the lake and surrounding land before there were cottages. They'd sent up soldiers from Trenton for war games and artillery tests. There were still pieces of old shells down at the bottom, if you knew where to look.

Dana seemed unimpressed. She asked for an introduction to the new man.

'This is my cousin, Marko,' said Andrew. 'He's visiting from Croatia. Just flew in yesterday.'

Marko gave a wave, and Dana reminded Andrew that she was Croatian, too.

'Well then, you should come over to the Pagoda tonight,' said Andrew. 'I'm throwing a party. The two of you can chat.'

Dana nodded when he suggested a time, then pushed off and paddled away. They all watched her go.

'She's something, isn't she?' said Andrew.

'Who is she?' asked Marko, still fingering the mortar shell.

'The girlfriend of the guy who owns the A-frame across the lake,' Andrew replied. 'She came by the Pagoda a couple of days ago, just after Tim and I arrived.'

'The guy had to leave on some emergency business trip, and she's stuck here waiting for him,' Tim added. 'I think she's lonely.'

Marko grinned, and Tim realized that what he'd said sounded like an insinuation. He hadn't meant it that way.

'How old do you think she is?' Marko asked. 'Thirty-five? Forty?'

Tim remembered Andrew saying that Marko was in his thirties; that he'd been their age when he'd started fighting in the war.

Andrew shrugged. 'She's too old for me and Timmy anyhow.' He smirked at Marko. 'Why? You interested?'

Marko smirked back but dropped his gaze.

'Two Croatians, what were the odds?' Andrew said. 'Maybe it was meant to happen.'

Marko grunted and did a back roll off the side of the boat.

In the next hour, he found two more shell pieces, and Andrew managed to drag up a small one of his own. They stayed longer than Tim would have liked, probably because Andrew was hoping for him to find a piece, too. The idea of searching for them had been Andrew's, just as he'd been the one to invite Tim up here for the week. Tim should have been grateful. He knew he wasn't fun to be around when he got into a rut like the one he'd been in this summer. But his head throbbed from the sun, and he only felt sorry for himself for not being able to appreciate someone's thoughtfulness and hospitality or even a swim in a lake on a hot day. It was a relief when Andrew announced that they needed to head back.

They were halfway to the dock when Marko finally took off his shirt. Trying to be inconspicuous, Tim looked at Marko's chest and arms. The only things of any note that he could see were two round inoculation scars below the left shoulder, one above the other like a light socket. He wasn't sure what he'd been expecting. Scars maybe. The tattoo of a platoon insignia. A chest wound that had never fully healed, one that shrank and grew as Marko breathed. Even that wouldn't have surprised Tim like the complete absence of anything remarkable did. Andrew had told him stories about what the man had been through, stuff to make you sick, and his skin offered nothing to corroborate them.

Tim was so taken aback that he didn't understand at first when the boat began to slow, the motor dying in pitch. They'd caught up to Dana in her canoe, and Andrew was easing them by her out of courtesy. She stopped paddling to look at them. Tim worried that she'd noticed him staring, but she wasn't looking at him. She was watching Marko, and he was meeting her eyes without smiling or blinking.

Andrew looked like he'd registered what was happening. At any moment, he'd say something; he had to. But he stayed silent.

Then he increased the speed, and Marko turned his attention to the sky.

'Might rain tonight,' he said.

Andrew had invited a bunch of his Engineering classmates and some buddies from his high school days to drive up and join them for the night. In the end, almost twenty of them showed up at the Pagoda. That was the name his family had given their cottage, which was octagonal and sat ten feet above the ground on a central concrete pedestal. When Andrew's parents had built it five years ago, they'd claimed the style of architecture was popular in California. Andrew said he'd overheard people at the local convenience store arguing about whether the building looked more like a spaceship or a tree fort. Cars on the lakeside road were always slowing down as they went by so that the passengers could gawk. Tonight, though, the partygoers' centre of attention was Marko and the mortar shells. The shells lay exhibited on the patio picnic table with some beach towels underneath them. Before the hamburgers were served, while everyone was still on their first beer, Marko gave a little lecture, explaining how the shells were fired, their ranges, their destructive capabilities, even the noises they made in the air.

'Not like that whistling sound in the movies,' he said. 'When they are coming at you, the sound is more like a bird flapping its wings.'

Tim frowned along with everyone else to show that he knew this was serious business. Nobody other than Marko spoke, as if they were all afraid to make a joke, say the wrong thing, ask a question that might lead to an awkward answer. As soon as Marko finished talking, they scattered, some to start a fire in the backyard pit, others to pick raspberries at the edge of the forest where the tree frogs were singing. Dana was the only one to approach Marko. Tim watched the two of them say a few words to each other. Then they headed down the driveway by themselves. Just before they vanished behind the trees, Marko touched her arm.

Tim wandered to the living room and sat on the couch, nursing a beer and watching people sort themselves into little circles of conversation. Andrew came and went, busy ensuring that things ran smoothly. He'd made four trips to the store that day, and in the morning, he'd driven to a farmer's stand out on the highway, so that in the bathroom right now, a watermelon was cooling in the tub, sparking laughter each time someone went in and saw it. Tim felt bad that he hadn't done more to help get ready for the party, but Andrew had insisted on doing almost everything. Tim also tried not to take it personally that Andrew had put so much effort into throwing a party when, during their year sharing a dorm room in Toronto, he'd never suggested hosting anything together. Tim could hardly blame him. Andrew had got stuck spending his first year at university with a roommate who was moody, taciturn, and prone to watching movies alone in the common room at all hours. In Andrew's place, Tim probably would have requested a change of dorms. At the very least, he'd have avoided becoming invested in the roommate's well-being. He certainly wouldn't have invited the roommate to his family's cottage for a week at a time of year when people were supposed to be enjoying themselves.

It was after dark when Marko and Dana returned from wherever they'd gone. By then, everyone had gathered in the dining room to play party games: Scissors, Psychiatrist, Magic Numbers, Black Magic. The room was illuminated by candles that Tim had lit – his one involvement in the preparations. At first, the ceiling fan had blown them all out, so Tim had turned it off before relighting them, and now the room was hot and shadowy. He sat on a chair in the corner, sucking at his beer. When they played Who'd I Shoot? he put his finger to his head as he said, 'Bang bang bang,' and Andrew shook his head with a tired smile. Then one of Andrew's high school friends, Julie, came in, dragging Dana by the hand.

'Guess what? She's going to tell our fortunes.' The zeal in Julie's voice implied that it had taken some convincing. 'She has the right blood for it. Her people lived in a caravan in the mountains.' From the look on Dana's face, Julie had to be making up that part.

They gathered around the table while Dana prepared for her performance. The deck of cards she brought out were from Croatia, she said. The suits were indecipherable: one with coin-like circles, one with shapes resembling truncheons, and one with things like flowerpots. The fourth was a vicious slash of parallel lines. She laid the cards face down in a grid before beginning to flip them over, two or three at a time, and gazing silently at what was revealed.

'Look at her concentration,' Andrew told the room. 'Julie, you've found the real deal.'

Julie's fortune came first. Straightaway, Dana told her that she would not retire until the age of sixty-eight. Julie shrugged; sixty-eight was a long way off.

Then Dana said that Julie would be pregnant six times but have only four children. At this, there was an outcry. Someone declared that you couldn't say that kind of thing. People made noises of agreement, but Tim stayed quiet. He hadn't realized that there were rules to this sort of game; that predictions could be negotiated; that the audience could demand retractions.

Dana seemed not to have known there were rules either. 'All right,' she said reluctantly. 'Pregnant six times, though. I'm sure.'

'What about her love life?' asked Andrew, as though to return them to safer territory.

'Yes, there's love,' Dana replied. 'No one escapes love.'

When she announced that Julie's fortune was finished, some-one said that Andrew should go next. Andrew blanched, and Julie asked him teasingly if something was wrong. He said that he wanted to know if there was a death card in the deck. He wouldn't do it if there was one.

'No,' said Dana. 'It's only a simple game. Trivial, for fun.'

Tim wondered where she'd learned the word *trivial*.

'All right,' said Andrew, sitting down across from Dana and rubbing his hands together. 'How many kids, and how much money will I make? Tell me the good stuff.'

She shook her head. It wasn't that simple. She could only say what the cards told her.

Still, by the end of her reading, he seemed happy with what she'd seen: a long life, good sex. She said that he was always trying to please people; that he must do more for himself, expand his horizons.

All the time she talked, Tim watched her flip the cards, trying to match them to what she said. There was no discernible pattern, no predictable reaction to any suit or number.

Then Julie suggested that she do Marko.

Dana shook her head. 'No, I couldn't. No, really.'

But Andrew must have been telling people about the two of them, or maybe it was just Dana's resistance that got people excited, because suddenly everyone was into the idea. She kept saying no, and they kept insisting. They pled theatrically, promised to make it worth her while, threatened to scuttle her canoe and not let her go home until she'd done it. They were all pretty drunk. The whole time, Marko stood against the wall with his eyes on the floor.

'All right,' said Dana finally.

She rearranged the deck, and they made Marko take Andrew's place opposite her. Then she began, never lifting her gaze from the cards. Some of the candles had burned out, so that Tim could no longer distinguish the cards' suits, and he could barely see Dana's face. As she spoke, he followed her voice alone.

The seven of *špade*. You have no cares about what people say or do to influence you. You have given up on understanding them. You want them to stop trying to understand you.

The ace of *kupe*. You have hurt people. You worry that you do not feel sorry enough. That you would hurt them again if given the choice. But choosing the same thing means you remain one person. It is a way of holding yourself together.

The two of *baštoni*, and the jack. There has been a woman. In a place you visited. An affair, in the middle of conflict. You made promises. You abandoned her. Many years ago now. You thought you would not see her again, not her or her family. Her parents. Her cousin. You have forgotten them. It was not serious to you. Your hands are clean. Your life seems distant and unreal.

The four of *dinari*. There. That's all. That's all I see.

Dana stood up and left the room. No one else moved. Their eyes were on Marko. Tim could feel the hum of rising energy. Then Andrew rocked back in his chair and exhaled loudly, and that seemed a signal for everyone to start asking Marko questions. Was it true? Had there been a woman? What happened to her? Was Dana the cousin?

Marko sat there with his beer in hand, peeling off the label. Tim wished that they would all go home. He wanted Marko to be left alone. He wanted to be alone, too. All the brunt of the day's sun seemed to be hitting him at once. He felt light-headed, dizzy. His eyes ached, his lips felt shrunken into his face, and his nostrils burned. Not even water would soothe him now; it would only taste hot and syrupy. He needed to escape to a pitch-black bedroom and lie down on cool sheets in absolute quiet.

Marko still hadn't spoken. He finished off his beer, then stood and started for the patio.

'Some people spend too much time imagining,' he said.

As soon as he was gone, the conversation broke into talk among smaller groups, everyone whispering. Tim leaned back against the wall and closed his eyes. Eventually, he heard the sounds of Andrew and a few others heading outside to smoke.

Not more than a minute passed before Andrew came back into the room.

'The sky is falling,' he announced. Nobody paid any attention until he explained: shooting stars. Meteors. Of course, said Julie, it was the Perseids shower, it happened every summer. But the rest decided to get excited, and they rushed to the patio. When Tim followed them, he found the space crowded with bodies on their backs, and it seemed there wasn't any room to lie down, until someone had the idea to climb to the roof.

The stars were everywhere, thick and soupy, except on the black fringes where the cedars crept into the sky. The only other light came from a few distant dock lamps. Up on the roof, Tim could make out the surface of the lake, reflecting the stars back at themselves. He lay down and unfocused his eyes to take in as much of the sky as possible. A few minutes passed before the first fireball streaked through his field of vision. All around him, people cried out at the sight. After that, every minute or so, if you were paying attention and your vision was sharp enough, you could witness the flickering interpenetration of heaven and Earth.

Most people kept their voices low, but Tim could hear Andrew on the other side of the roof, improvising a story about what would happen if a meteor landed in the lake. A shock wave; a cloud of steam; a wall of water washing away everyone on the patio, while the people on the roof were saved.

'He is talking shit,' murmured someone close to Tim. It was Marko, lying beside him.

'Pretty much,' said Tim. He searched for something else to say. 'The light show's spectacular, though, right? Do you have this in Croatia?'

Marko gave a little grunt. 'Of course. We call it *suze svetog Lovre* – the tears of Saint Lawrence.'

'Why?' Tim said.

'Because this is the time of year when he was put to death.'

Tim didn't know how to respond. Finally, he was granted relief by a meteor that flared halfway across the sky, earning whoops and cheers. Then the night was quiet again but for the tree frogs, and for all he could tell, he and Marko were the only two people in the world.

'You believe what she said about me?' said Marko after a time.

Tim felt his pulse quicken. 'Dana? No – why? It's not true, is it?'

Marko took a long time in replying.

'I don't know,' he said.

'What do you mean?' Tim's voice came out higher than he wanted it to.

Marko sighed. Then he began to talk. Everything she had accused him of was so general, so vague. During the fighting, those kinds of things had happened all the time. Many men, many women, everyone caught in a bad time. He'd talked with her on their walk; all was fine until she asked about the war. He should have been more careful, but he'd got carried away, been too specific. He hadn't thought it would make a problem. He didn't remember any cousin.

'What will you do now?' Tim asked.

Marko snorted. 'Nothing. What should I do?'

'I don't know. Go after her.'

'No. Not worth it. I leave in a few days. I was just seeing how far I could get.'

Tim scanned from left to right without success. No meteors. The sky had gone dead. His mind crossed the ocean, travelled back a decade. An image came into focus like a shot in a movie: Marko marching through a bombed-out town, his uniform declaring his devotion to a cause.

'What's it like?' Tim found himself saying. 'You know. Killing someone.'

There was silence. He imagined Marko seething, tensing, preparing to stand up and throw him off the roof.

Then Marko's voice came, slow and quiet. 'It was no big deal, after a while.'

'Really?' Tim tried to swallow, but his throat was too dry. 'I don't think I could bring myself to do something like that.'

'You could,' said Marko. 'Anybody can.'

Most people who'd gone up to the roof were still there when Tim climbed back down. He went to his room, stripped to nothing, and lay on the bed. It was a proper old-school cottage bed, with a creaky wooden frame and a lumpy, lopsided mattress, out of place in such a new building. From above came the sound of footsteps and laughter and, twice, breaking glass.

Then he heard noises from the bathroom on the other side of the wall. The running of tap water; the roll of the toilet-paper dispenser. Two women's voices. He couldn't make out what they were saying, but one of them he recognized as Dana's. When the other voice grew louder, he realized it was Julie's, kind and harsh and condescending at the same time. It's all right now. He's on the roof. Pull yourself together.

In the mind's eye of sleep, Tim is still at the Pagoda, but all the guests have disappeared. Outside, it's absolutely dark. The windows are closed and the ceiling fan thrums. Tim is looking for everyone. He searches the entire house, even the closets and cupboards, under the beds. No sign. He's afraid that he'll have to go outside to find them. Animal eyes watch through the windows. Then he awakens and begins sorting dream from reality. He's still uncertain about some things when he hears knocking and sees Marko in the doorway.

'Get up. We are going after her.'

Tim dresses, and they pass silently through the house. Someone's lying on the couch, anonymous within the ruffle of a sleeping bag. The floor is littered with cans and bottles. So is the ground beneath the Pagoda. The sun hasn't quite risen. In the time it takes them to reach the path to the lake, Marko tells him what Julie has said: that Dana left sometime after four. She said she was going home in the canoe. The A-frame doesn't have a telephone, and Julie is worried. When Marko asked her to describe these worries, she couldn't bring herself to answer. She only insisted that Dana was upset.

'Why did Julie ask you to go instead of someone else?' Tim asks.

'Because I am not as drunk as the others.'

'Why do I need to come, too?'

Marko shrugs. 'Because you are not as drunk as I am.'

The path down to the shoreline is rocky and slick with dew. Marko has fallen into silence, as if steeling himself for some great rescue: strangling a rattlesnake with his bare hands; mouth-to-mouth resuscitation. The lake is too narrow to permit certain lines of fantasy: when they arrive at the dock, they can see Dana's canoe pulled up on the far shore. They can't see Dana, though. The A-frame is over there waiting for them, dark and lonely, nestled in fairy-tale forest. There isn't a breath of wind, and the water lies still, reflecting pre-dawn colours.

The motor is sleepy and slow to start. Tim has been instructed in operating the boat but has never actually driven it. Marko's the one who knows what to do with the gas tanks, squeezing tubes and loosening caps. He takes the wheel and guides them away from the dock.

Halfway across the lake, Tim calls out for Marko to slow down. Something is floating in the water. Tim goes to the bow and snags it with the net, brings it into the boat, and takes it into his hand. It's a playing card.

'Look,' he says, pointing not to the card but to the lake.

They lie flat and motionless ahead: the rest of Dana's cards, strung out in a long trail that suggests they weren't scattered all at once but were set down deliberately, one by one. The sun has just begun to edge over the trees, and it makes the cards flash like knives. They're spaced so evenly that if you were quick enough and light enough, you might hop from one to the other all the way across the lake. An invitation or a warning: it's impossible to tell.

The two of them go along slowly, Tim at the bow with the net, calling directions to Marko and scooping out the cards until they have half the pack. They begin to weave around to pick up strays. Sometimes Tim fumbles and misses one, or Marko speeds up at the wrong time, and soon enough they're laughing and flinging water at each other with the bailing buckets and calling one another assholes. With the sun up, nothing seems serious anymore. In the back of Tim's mind, he knows where they're headed, but they're following a mutual impulse, an instinct for play, until finally they're at the jagged edge of the lake where the reeds cluster, ready to choke a motor. They're so much into their game that they've forgotten all the other rules, and Marko almost drives onto shore until Tim yells at him to stop.

They drift beside the vegetation. Tim feels suddenly confused. There's a compulsion to do something, anything, to resume the game before the laughter and exhilaration are gone for good. They need to be perpetuated, climaxed, if just for a second.

Tim can think of only one thing. With a sweep of his arm, he throws all the cards over the side of the boat.

Three or four make it as far as the reeds, but most of them catch on the air and flutter down in front of him, a few landing on the deck. His gut flips with unfulfilment. He picks up the cards at his feet and throws them overboard again. One of them falls back into the boat once more, and he swipes it viciously from the wet fibreglass, crumples it, and hurls it away.

When he turns, his breath quick and shallow, he freezes. Marko has been watching him silently. Now, with Tim's eyes on him, Marko starts to laugh: a low chuckle from the back of his throat, like he's been waiting for Tim to make just such a mistake, as though Marko has kept his head and known the right thing to do all along. Tim recognizes that laugh. It's the way in which you're supposed to finish these kinds of games. It's the way in which you win.

THE THUNBERG PLEDGE

By this point, everyone has heard of the Thunberg Pledge and what it asks of you. On Facebook, the pledge has been shared nearly half a million times. Countless pundits have praised or denounced it. The author of the pledge has stayed anonymous, preferring to let it speak for itself. Yet the first time I read the thing, it seemed like somebody I knew was whispering the words. Later, I felt stupid for not recognizing her voice.

Many people still assume that the creator of the Thunberg Pledge is Greta Thunberg, even though, after the pledge went viral, Thunberg declared that she had nothing to do with it. Since then, she has been lukewarm in her assessment of the document, insisting that the changes it seeks require action by governments and corporations, not just individuals. Still, the Thunberg Pledge has gained legions of devotees.

One result is that several variants now exist online. The original version, however, remains the most frequently shared.

The Thunberg Pledge

Because we owe future generations a world free from the ravages of anthropogenic climate change, because the crisis is urgent, and because we can solve it while still enjoying happy lives, I make this commitment:

1. *I won't eat beef or dairy.*
2. *I won't go on cruises or fly to vacation.*
3. *If travelling, I'll walk, bike, or take mass transit when possible.*
4. *I'll avoid buying new goods when I can fix old ones or buy used ones.*
5. *If I own a vehicle, I'll keep it as long as it will run. Then, should I still need to drive, I'll buy a hybrid or electric car if I can afford it.*
6. *I'll vote for politicians with credible platforms to reduce carbon emissions. When possible, I'll donate time and money to their campaigns.*
7. *I'll have no more than one child (or no more children if I'm already a parent).*

None of the points is unique to the pledge; before its creation, there were plenty of books and articles on how to tackle the climate crisis. But few insisted that people commit to anything, and it was rare to demand such personal austerity.

Maybe the Thunberg Pledge is so popular because it's so demanding. In the face of a problem that has developed over generations and been greeted by world leaders with half measures, inaction, even mockery, the Thunberg Pledge reassures people that they can make a difference all by themselves.

There are, by now, many parodies of the pledge. There's also a subreddit, r/thunbergpledgecheatday, that's devoted to people's accounts of activities such as renting monster trucks and hosting family reunions at Arby's. When I first saw this subreddit, I couldn't help but wonder what the pledge's author would think. Reporters' efforts to identify the person had failed, but I didn't have much going on, so I decided to see if I could find her.

And yes, I assumed she was a woman. Later, I admitted to myself that I was pretty sure I knew exactly who she was. A preposterous idea, and no less so when I turned out to be right.

Of the pledge's origins, all anyone could say for certain was that the thing had first been posted November 18, 2022, on Facebook. The earliest known people to share it claimed they'd found it on an environmentalist group's page, but if the pledge had once existed there, it had been deleted, and Meta declined my request to look into the matter.

With no leads or journalistic bona fides, just a niggling impulse, I started lurking on climate-change discussion boards, reasoning that if the pledge's author had launched her creation online, she might return there to defend it. What I found were hundreds of people endlessly debating the pledge's points.

Take the one-child commitment. People have called it the pledge's poison pill. More folks than you'd think are, it turns out, desperate to have multiple kids. A typical Reddit comment: *Why should I be allowed only one mini-me when people in some parts of the world have seven or eight?* Never mind that a child in the West leaves ten times the carbon footprint of one in a developing country.

Then there's the ban on vacation flights. Some people think that the pledge should prohibit air travel entirely, but a lot of twentysomethings balk at being told that they're not allowed to see the world, especially when their friends have been Insta-gramming the hell out of Oahu. And there are the baby boomers who can't fathom abandoning their winters in Fort Lauderdale. A few of them, approaching the pledge in a literalist manner, have declared that spending a season someplace doesn't count as a vacation.

Such lines of argument are an indication of how the Thunberg Pledge has become a kind of sacred text, its meanings as carefully parsed and hotly contested as those of the Bible or the US Constitution. Online debates about its creator's intentions made me all the keener to find her and ask her what she'd meant.

I first encountered u/janell@doog on the subreddit for the Voluntary Human Extinction Movement, which is, in fact, a real thing. The username kept appearing in threads about the Thunberg Pledge's implications for the movement, the aims of which are summed up by its title. Most participants in the forum are big fans of species suicide, so they don't appreciate the pledge's support of reproduction, even if it limits people to one child. The pro-extinction types concede that universal adherence to the pledge would lead to the end of humankind eventually, but they don't like how long it would take.

In this crowd, u/janell@doog stood out as one of the pledge's most stalwart advocates. But what really caught my eye was her vocabulary. At one point, she said that unconscious drives in human beings were 'ineliminable.' At another, she claimed that the pledge's supporters 'supernumerated' its critics. She stressed the importance of 'turning velleities into praxis.' She accused her interlocutors of 'muzzy thinking' and 'noisome ructions.' She dismissed alternative versions of the pledge as 'cagmags,' 'gallimaufries,' and 'slumgullions.' More than once, she was asked who'd given her the Word-of-the-Day calendar. But while her vocabulary distinguished her, she never posted details about herself.

For my part, I was sure I knew her. In my life, only one person had ever used the word *cagmag* in conversation and, as it happened, the same individual had once written me a flirty email asking if my desire to see her again was 'a mere velleity.' I thought of calling her, but it had been a long time. I decided to seek more evidence.

It didn't take long. In the Ecology forum on Craigslist, I found a frequent commenter, yessofn@ID, with the same hypertrophied vocabulary. On the EcoLink discussion board, a user called 1lewd@ertmit had one, too. Like u/janell@doog, they were both loyal defenders of the Thunberg Pledge.

On a hunch, I went to Google Scholar and typed in some of their more highfalutin words, looking for a magic bullet, an article featuring a gem such as *vitiate* or *nullifidian*. It turns out that academics use these words more often than you'd think. Even when I limited my search to the past year, there were almost six thousand hits for *otiose* and over five thousand for *recrudesce*.

Then I entered another of u/janell@doog's words: *titivation*. To my amazement, there were only eighteen results. Among them was a chemistry article, published the previous year, on the enzymatic biodegradation of terephthalate-glycol bonds. Even before I checked the byline, I knew who the author was. Hardly proof of anything, but enough for me.

I decided to forego a phone call. After lunch, I made sure there was no bus route leading to her place, so I wouldn't feel bad about driving there. Then I tried to sleep a little, wanting to be rested for the trip. The past few months, too much time spent alone at home pondering my fortunes and the planet's had led to high levels of baseline anxiety, and the anxiety had given rise to insomnia, and the insomnia had necessitated catnaps. That afternoon, when I closed my eyes, I fell into the same fretful dreams that had been plaguing me for weeks: visions of burning jungles, beached whales, ice shelves calving into pea-soup seas. I know from social media that such nightmares are common now. They're our way of processing the crisis, preparing ourselves for what's ahead.

After half an hour, I woke and slid out of bed, shaved, and put on a sweater she'd once bought me. Then I got in the car.

The house was an hour outside the city, a modest bungalow in a well-established suburb, the kind of neighbourhood where the biggest daily menace is a deer nibbling your begonias, and where everybody at the tennis club opts for the lifetime membership. I'd been there only once before, a couple of years back, right after she moved in, dropping by at her request to pick up a bread machine that I'd relinquished in the split but that she suddenly, for some reason, couldn't stand to be around. The visit ended with me squealing the tires as I left her driveway, the bread machine abandoned on the lawn. I thought of going back to explain that I hadn't accelerated hard on purpose, I was just upset, but I kept driving, and we hadn't spoken since.

I'm embarrassed to admit that when I turned up at her door two years later to confront her about the Thunberg Pledge, I didn't recognize the person who answered. The pixie cut threw me. Also, she wore tights and a T-shirt, though it was mid-December and snowing. Her cheeks were gaunt, and the skin beneath her eyes sagged. God knows how I looked to her.

'Tim,' she said. 'What are you doing here?'

As she spoke, her face changed into that of the person I remembered. Ada. The cropped hair and lost weight felt like a betrayal, at once an attempt to deceive me and a disowning of the person she'd been when we were together. I thought of commenting on her haircut, but I decided to stick to the opening I'd concocted during the drive.

'I'm here about the Thunberg Pledge,' I said.

Ada's expression was enough. She didn't seem shocked, which maybe I'd hoped for, or even angry, which I'd expected. There was just sadness. Her hand twitched on the door.

'Huh,' she said. 'I thought you might figure it out.'

That took me by surprise. 'How come?' I said.

'Because we had a conversation about it. Remember?'

I didn't remember.

'That night at Il Pegno,' she said. 'You wrote our ideas on a napkin.'

The detail set off a spark, but dimly.

What I remembered was that it had been our third anniversary – our final one, although I didn't know it then. I remembered worrying about the sadistic dearth of vegetarian options, and about whether the parking meter would run out, and about the possibility that, at some point in the meal, she would declare our marriage over. It had been a hard year. I'd been struggling to write; some days, to get out of bed. There'd been yelling at walls. She'd done her best, but I'd worn her out. Usually, we dealt with the situation by talking about any other subject. Our favourite thing was to imagine some project together – an app, a cookbook, a podcast – and brainstorm how it would go. Probably, the napkin with the pledge ideas had got left in my pocket and disintegrated in the wash.

'You're telling me we came up with the pledge?' I said.

'Well, it was mostly me. You were the amanuensis. You really don't remember?'

I shook my head. There's a lot of stuff from those years I don't recall, though they weren't that long ago.

'So, tell me again why you're here?' she said.

I didn't have an answer.

She glanced over her shoulder, then swung the door further open and motioned for me to enter. 'It's freezing out. You'd better come in if we're going to do this.'

'Do what?'

'Talk.'

'Talk about what?'

'I don't know. Whatever you drove here to talk about.'

After I took off my coat and shoes, she led me into the kitchen. The kettle she filled wasn't the one I remembered. The house looked different, too. When she'd moved in, there had been cracked linoleum, seventies shag in the adjacent living room, and dark wood panelling. Now, I saw new windows, hardwood floors, walls painted eggshell white.

'I know, I know,' she said, without me having uttered a word. 'It would have been greener to leave things. But the shabbiness was getting to me, and I thought I should commit to a life here.' She plugged in the kettle and frowned. 'This is exactly what I was afraid of. Being found out, then having to justify every little choice.' She turned to me with narrowed eyes. 'Are you writing about me and the pledge? For a magazine or something?'

'Don't be silly,' I replied.

Her eyes stayed narrowed. She reached for a pair of mugs and asked how I'd figured out it was her. I recapped what I'd done, low balling how much time I'd spent online.

'Sounds like stalking,' she said.

'It wasn't,' I protested. Then I realized she was joking. 'Anyhow, you're the one using aliases to argue with trolls.'

She shrugged. 'Yeah, well, I want the pledge to take off.'

'It's taking off fine,' I said. 'You've started a movement.'

To my surprise, she broke into a smile. 'I guess I have, haven't I?'

The pride in her voice was another new thing. I'd always known her as someone without an ego. She'd never fought to be first author on a paper, never scrabbled to lead a lab. One of her colleagues once told me how she did little things every day at work to encourage mutual care. At the time, I took it as a veiled rebuke, a hint that she'd told him how useless I was at home.

'For a while, before I wrote the pledge, I was online every night,' she said. 'I mean, I'm still online too much. But back then, I was tearing my hair out over people posting Earth Day memes right next to photos from their holidays in Cancún. I wanted to do something.'

The way she said it made me wonder if her research wasn't going well; if she knew, or at least suspected, that her project would never pan out.

A second later, there was a squawk in the living room. It came from a gadget on the coffee table, white and wallet-sized, with a stubby antenna and a tiny screen.

'Hey, what's that?' I said, like an idiot. I really hadn't been sleeping much.

The two of us had met seven years earlier in Montreal, at a conference called the Two Cultures Symposium. She worked in a lab looking for enzymes that would break down plastic, making it easier to recycle. I'd just finished a screenplay, and I didn't know what to write next. The conference was supposed to be a chance to find ideas. The two of us were randomly assigned places beside each other at the banquet, where the scientist-artist-scientist-artist seating arrangement brutishly enforced the conference's theme. In the first five minutes of conversation, she used the words 'pinchbeck,' 'propinquity,' and 'discommodious.' Only after half an hour did we discover that we worked at the same Toronto university, though its name had been on our conference badges the whole time.

Back home, I visited her lab. She read my screenplay. We moved in together, got married, wrote our own vows. She kept her name. We stuck with condoms. I started writing a screenplay about a mid-life crisis. Then I started writing a screenplay about the war in the former Yugoslavia. Then I started writing a screenplay about a woman from Upstate New York who works in a lab looking for enzymes to break down plastic. She was patient with me, but in 2019, I agreed to sign the divorce papers.

For a few months, we tried being friends. She still worked in the lab. I still led workshops up the street. I began writing a screenplay about a divorced grocer. Then, once the pandemic hit, I began writing a novel about a divorced endocrinologist who gets reincarnated as a chimp. I had more success with that one. A hundred pages in, I started jogging and getting up before noon. Not long afterward, without anything to signal a change between us, we fell out of touch. At first, I assumed it was my fault. Only later did I wonder if she'd met someone else.

Excusing herself from the kitchen, she went to the living room and checked the gadget on the coffee table. Then she headed down the corridor leading to the rest of the house. The kettle began to scream. I switched it off. A second later, I realized what the gadget on the coffee table was. My hands started trembling a little.

When she reappeared with the kid in her arms, I gave him a once-over. There was a tuft of black hair, a standard-issue baby mouth, and eyes that were anime versions of hers. Five months old, maybe six. No way was he mine.

'Say hello,' she said, and I didn't know whether she was addressing the baby or me.

'Hello,' I said softly.

He rubbed his eyes with doughy knuckles.

'Jesus, you didn't know, did you?' she said. 'Don't hate me. I was going to tell you – '

'So you're on leave from the lab, or what?'

She sighed and jounced the baby. 'Sure.'

The kid hadn't yet deigned to look my way.

'The father isn't in the picture,' she said. 'My folks visit pretty often to help out. You just missed my stepmom.'

'Too bad,' I said. Her stepmom had always hated me. 'So, where's the father?' I meant 'who,' but I said 'where.'

'Long gone,' she replied. Then, as if she suddenly understood my concern, she added, 'I mean, he wasn't on the scene until after you and me – '

'That's good,' I said.

I stood there raging. We'd been so careful not to have a child. We'd been so wholly in agreement about not wanting one. About procreation being a moral failure.

'Would you give me a hand?' she said.

I followed her into the living room. Pointing to a woollen blanket on the couch, she asked me to spread it across the floor. Then she set the baby on it. I expected him to protest at being left there, but he babbled happily, kicking his little legs.

From a plastic crate beside the couch, she produced a stuffed koala, a beaded bracelet, and a palm-sized mirror in a wooden frame. After she'd positioned them at various points around the blanket, we sat down to watch him. He rolled onto his back and stretched a leg until his socked toes were in his mouth.

'So – a baby,' I said.

She mm-hmmed, her eyes fixed on the child.

'You weren't going to tell me?'

'I thought someone else would.'

'Who? After the divorce, everyone dropped me.'

The baby rocked himself side to side until he was on his stomach again, in range of the bracelet, which he picked up and shook with a terrier's vigour. The beads clinking made him laugh. His laughter made me laugh, too, despite myself. She hadn't told me his name.

'He seems fun,' I said.

She nodded. 'Eats like a champ. Sleeping on his own is trickier. Isn't it, buddy?'

Just the sight of him was soothing: the way he gave his attention wholly to the bracelet, then the mirror, then his foot again. It occurred to me that it must be a nice change for her, sharing life with someone who was all potential. No false starts yet, no compounding regret and melancholic sulks.

'Was he planned?' I asked.

'Let's not go there.'

'Did you tell the father?'

When she didn't reply, I looked around the room. It was so spare. No messes, no clutter. I figured that everything had to be jammed in the crate beside the couch.

'How's the writing going?' she asked. 'Still at it?'

I nodded. 'Sorry to disappoint you.'

'What do you mean?'

'You once called me a graphomaniac.'

'Only because I knew you'd like the word.'

She was right; I'd loved it. She'd done that all the time: flexed her vocabulary to weaken my knees.

She cooed to the baby, reached to adjust one of his socks. As I watched, it came to me that parenting together was something we would have enjoyed. We could have made a new person and helped him grow. She would have cut back her hours at the lab. I would have stopped caring so much about making a name for myself. I'd have appreciated the routine of parenthood, the satisfaction of simple things accomplished: a bottle warmed, a lullaby sung. I'd have relished noticing the tiny, daily changes as the kid went from grub to tyke to teenager. I saw it all so clearly that I found myself bewildered as to why it hadn't happened.

Then I remembered.

'You used to think it was selfish to become a parent,' I said.

She let out a breath. 'Do we have to go into this?'

'You used to say there wasn't a single good reason. You said adoption was the only ethical choice.'

'Yes, I did.' Her lips tightened.

'I should have guessed when I saw the pledge,' I said. 'The one-child policy.'

'It isn't there for my sake. It's for people who – '

'It wasn't you wimping out? Your folks finally getting to you?'

She stood up. 'You should go. He's due for a feeding.'

I didn't move. She crossed her arms. Beneath me, the couch grew hot and lumpish. From his blanket, he reached for her, making little huffs of impatience. I rose and went to the door.

As I finished putting on my shoes, she came over, holding him.

'You know, I took the pledge,' I said. 'Last month.'

'I know. I saw your post on Facebook.'

'I fixed my old bike. I'm going to try riding all winter.'

She raised her eyebrows. 'Well, good for you.'

I opened the door. As I was deciding whether I should offer to hug her, she stepped forward and put her free arm around me. The baby was between us, his head just below my face. My nostrils filled with the scent of talcum. On instinct, I lay a quick, light kiss on his tufted scalp.

She pulled back and smoothed down his hair, as if trying to erase what I'd done.

'Say goodbye to Uncle Tim,' she told him.

I didn't want to be Uncle Tim. I wanted to keep talking with her, but I was standing with the door open, and the baby started to paw at her, and snow blew wetly onto her new floor, so I stepped outside.

Driving home, I swore at SUVs going too fast on the slippery highway. I tutted self-righteously at a BMW abandoned in the ditch. When a pickup truck came up behind me, flashing its brights, I refused to budge from the passing lane.

I had long thought that adulthood involved a choice: devote your life to making something of yourself or devote yourself to kids. I'd chosen myself, thinking that if only I learned to use words the right way, then one day I might help to change the world.

Now, her words had found a bigger audience than mine ever would. They were transforming people's lives.

All that, and a baby, too.

I came home to a cold apartment, having turned down the thermostat before going out. Reducing home energy use wasn't part of the Thunberg Pledge, but some people thought it should be. I recalled what u/janell@doog had written on the matter: *Aren't people already using less home energy? It's like recycling. Why make them promise to do what they're already doing?* Then I remembered how Ada's house had been warm enough for her to go around in a T-shirt. Had she even taken the pledge? How could she justify living so far from her lab? Moving to that house had seemed an obvious attempt to put distance on me, or at least on her sense of responsibility for my wellness. I tried to imagine her raising a baby there on her own. I told myself that her looking me up on Facebook didn't mean anything.

That night, I craved ribs but settled for takeout pizza with fake cheese. After two slices and three beers, I phoned her.

'You got home all right?' she asked, sounding liked she'd expected me to call.

I said I had. Then I asked how long her leave was scheduled to last.

'Six months,' she said. 'Why?'

'I was thinking, if you want help, I could babysit.'

'Oh,' she said. 'That's thoughtful of you.'

'I'm still in the condo. I teach on Tuesdays, but otherwise I'm home most of the time. You could drop him off and pick him up whenever you like. Or I could drive there, if that's easier.'

'Thanks,' she said. 'Thanks for offering.'

I listened to silence eat the line.

'So that's a no, then,' I said. 'Too weird?'

'Yeah. Too weird.'

'Listen, can I ask you one more thing?'

In the background, the baby started wailing.

'What's the top reason you'd give for why our marriage didn't work out?' I asked.

'Oh God.'

'I don't need a disquisition. Just whatever comes to mind.'

The baby's crying wouldn't stop.

'I have to go,' she said. 'I'll call you back.'

'Okay. I'll be up late.'

She didn't call. I checked her Facebook: no new posts. I checked EcoLink, Reddit, and Craigslist, along with a few other sites in case she'd moved camp. Nothing. I tried to sleep, but whenever I started to drift off, I fell into the usual dreams. Meltwater laced with ocean salt. The heat of the Santa Ana winds. Frogs singing threnodies in parched fens. Without getting up, I grabbed my phone and returned to lurking on Reddit.

It was two in the morning when the email arrived, lacking a subject line and sent from a Hotmail address I didn't recognize, so that I almost deleted the thing before realizing who'd written it.

Tim,

You asked for a reason. How about the fact that you never wanted to leave the house or spend time with people, and you got upset when I wanted to? Have you considered how hard it was for me to go anywhere, given the state you were in?

How about all the talk? I'd come back from work and listen to you lay out, seriatim, half a dozen ideas you'd had for your latest script, and then I'd sit through your postmortem of the book you were reading or the film you'd just watched, and nothing impressed you, everything was junk, and the opprobrium got more and more outrageous, until I figured you just wanted me to soothe you. It occurs to me now, though, that maybe you were looking for pushback. Maybe whatever composure I managed was only exasperating you.

With a baby, when he's hungry, you feed him. When his diaper's wet, you change it. I never knew what you wanted. You'd say you were fine and stew all day. You'd talk a big game politically, and then, when it came to taking action, you always had a hundred reasons not to.

That's a grubby thing for me to say, but I won't delete it, because I want you to appreciate that I was trying to give you an honest answer just now. I wasn't trying to ingratiate myself before asking you what I'm about to ask.

First, though, I should tell you: I originally shared the Thunberg Pledge on Facebook under my own name. You know what happened? In the first hour, I got three likes and one comment that read: 'Is this for real?' I was so mortified, I deleted the post.

What I'm saying is, please don't tell anybody about me and the pledge. It has a life without me; it doesn't need me now. If you feel a compulsion to write about any of this, at least change the details. Make me a man, or a dental hygienist, or Norwegian, okay? Will you do that for me?

– Ada

During our marriage, she always seemed to maintain such equanimity. Even when she announced that we were done, she didn't blame me. She just said the relationship had asked too much of her.

After another beer, I started writing a reply. I wanted to articulate my wish that I'd been different for her. I wanted her to know how the happiest I'd been in a long time was the day I'd taken the Thunberg Pledge. How, it was true, maybe I'd done it with hopes of her seeing the post, but I'd decided it didn't matter, because the planet didn't care what people's reasons were. I wanted to tell her how, for a moment, I'd finally seemed solid, real, no longer hovering apart, but an actual person taking an actual stance. I wanted to say that I'd never felt anything as soft as her son's hair against my lips.

The cursor on my laptop screen stayed idle. I knew what would happen if I sent such an email. I'd spend a week waiting for her to answer. She wouldn't respond. In the new year, I'd teach my classes and watch two movies a night, subsisting on a diet of beer and fake-cheese pizza, mulling whether to write about her creation of the Thunberg Pledge.

It seemed obvious that the only respectable thing was not to breathe a word. I owed that much to her – or, if not to her, then to the version of her with whom I'd spent four years. If I could be more like she was, a moral and upstanding person, keeping my mouth shut would have been straightforward.

It's tricky, though, when things are hard, to keep oneself from doing what's easy. And writing about your life is simple. Don't let anybody tell you otherwise. The material is right there, raw and glistening. There can be pain in it, like picking at a scab, but for some people, what's difficult is leaving it alone. Autobiography has the ease of talking to yourself, but with the benefits of a backspace key and the prerogative to throw a tarp over certain facts, stretch the truth, until your life becomes half-decent, something you can bear. You inch yourself closer to the human being you want to be, the sort of person Greta Thunberg might approve of.

I trust I'm not telling you anything new. So, nobody's opinion of me will change much if I say that this whole time, I haven't quite been honest; that I've made up some details.

For one thing, Ada isn't a scientist.

Also, her name isn't quite Ada.

And the Thunberg Pledge does not exist.

At least, that's not what it's called. I may have exaggerated its popularity, too. I may have made false claims about Greta Thunberg's awareness of it. You can, if you choose, go online to figure out how much I've lied.

I'll tell you this, at least: a few weeks ago, after another sleepless night on social media, half-drunk, scrolling through people's glossy posts about their blithe, beautiful, planet-killing lives, I first happened upon the real version of the Thunberg Pledge. It had been posted anonymously, but I knew she had to be the author. The tip-off was the vocabulary in the follow-up posts defending it – and the fact that I remembered the night with her long ago at Il Pegno. Somewhere in a box in my bedroom closet, I still have the napkin.

I was so excited by the pledge having entered the world, and so impressed by her having posted it, that I started to imagine writing a book that would advocate for the pledge to be adopted by everyone. And you know what? For a time, entertaining that idea, I felt happy. If I could publish such a book, I might make a difference, too.

Then the doubts crept in. The manuscript would take years to finish. If it was ever published, people would accuse me of exploiting her ideas. Probably, some MAGA jerk would end up doxxing me. Some parent to eight kids would send me death threats. What would I do then? I didn't even have another person to commiserate with. Once I'd foreseen these possibilities, the whole venture seemed too daunting, worthless, doomed to fail.

I knew, too, that she didn't want or need to hear from me.

So, you can rest easy. I took the simple way out. I made up everything. As far as I'm aware, nobody of my acquaintance has actually committed to the tenets of the Thunberg Pledge – nobody other than me, at least, and maybe one other person. The world is fine and will persist.

Though it's true, at least, about the dreams. Also, I don't have kids. I don't know how many she has.

THE STRESS OF LIVES

On the evening of March 15, 1983, the celebrated Hungarian-Canadian endocrinologist Hans Selye was reincarnated in Montreal as a young chimpanzee. To be reborn an ape is ordinarily no more remarkable than finding oneself a hedgehog or tsetse fly, but fate had seen fit to reincarnate Hans Selye as a very particular chimpanzee: one in the care of his wife, Lena. Or rather, until his rebirth it was the chimp's mother who was in Lena's care. The female chimp's pregnancy passed unnoticed, because Lena was consumed by grief over the recent death of Hans Selye and quite unaware of the world. Then, on March 15, out came Hans Selye in a fit of screaming and an expulsion of orange slime.

Hans Selye's mother did not last much longer in this world, the birth having complications for the mother-chimp that went unnoticed by Lena and untreated by any veterinarian. In truth, Lena's care for the mother had always been ambivalent. The mother was known to have been Hans Selye's favourite animal at his laboratory, and he had kept her long past the end of her scientific usefulness. After his death, one of Selye's colleagues mentioned to Lena that this favoured chimp would shortly be euthanized. The colleague had intuited Lena's resentment of the animal and anticipated her pleasure at the news. However, the thought of a second death was anathema to her, and she insisted on taking the animal home.

Caring for the mother-chimp was another matter. The problem for Lena wasn't only the odour and nightly harangues from the cage in the living room. It was the thought that during Hans Selye's long hours in his laboratory over the past decades, this creature had enjoyed more of his companionship than Lena had. Her and Lena's shared occupancy of Hans Selye's house grew to seem a gross mistake on Lena's part. Lena wouldn't have been able to articulate her feelings as such, but having to provide for the chimp, to clean her feces from the walls and endure her hooting, was more than Lena could bear.

The baby chimp, when he came, was a different case. Lena decided that he looked not a little like Hans Selye, so that although she didn't recognize the chimp as her reincarnated husband, she treated him almost as her husband's child. Eventually, when visitors called on Lena in her mourning – colleagues and admirers of the old professor who felt obliged to look in on his widow, people who had only ever seen her as an accessory to him and now found her to be a reassuring, if somewhat piteous, artifact of the great man's legacy – these guests were startled to discover that Lena had named the baby chimp Hans and that she doted on him without apology or shame.

Being a chimp, Hans didn't fully apprehend the fact of his reincarnation. He knew he had a bond with Lena that echoed, if not outstripped, his connection to his dead mother. Even if the gift of human voice had been bestowed upon him, though, he would not have said, 'I am Hans Selye, reincarnated as a little chimp in the care of my former wife.' He would only have said something like, 'I have a sense of recurrence, as though this form is not my only one, and this woman has recurred with me.' Still, such was his sense of kinship with Lena that he failed to register her as belonging to a different species. She was only the chimp who made strange noises, while he was the chimp with sharper nails.

As he grew, Hans came into a habit whereby he offered bits of green apple to Lena, bitten off in ragged chunks and handed to her on a leathery palm. This habit surprised her, because her husband Hans Selye had also liked to present her with slices of green apple, balanced at the end of a paring knife while they ate dessert and he dissected his fruit with laboratorial exactitude. Indeed, often he had brought apples home from the lab, where they were regularly delivered in bulk for the chimps' delectation. As it was part of Lena's upbringing always to accept gifts graciously, she had eaten these slices whenever her husband tendered them, but in truth she abominated green apples, and over the years she had gained a resentment of Hans for offering them without appreciating that she took them merely out of politeness. So, when the chimp Hans Selye offered her chunks of green apple, she did not think, 'Ah! This is my dead husband reincarnated, offering me bits of green apple as he once did!' She only thought, 'It is my misfortune to be living with a chimp who is as ignorant of my desires as Hans was.' But at the same time, when caring for the young chimp seemed too great a burden and she considered surrendering him to a zoo, she thought, 'It would be unkind, because then he would no longer have anyone to accept his offerings of green apple,' and this anticipation of his sadness made her resolve that they must continue together.

Some nights, Lena wept and screamed in bed, still stricken by her husband's absence. Hearing her from the living room was a sorrow to the chimp Hans Selye, who didn't know she mourned his former self, but who had some inkling that his own presence was a catalyst for her grief, even though she herself didn't apprehend this fact, just as a person with a fungal growth on the back of his neck might feel a dreadful itching but fail to perceive its origin, though everyone else can see it clearly. Hans Selye could sense his aggravation of Lena because animals do not have the luxury, as humans do, of ignoring their effects on fellow creatures. It is only through attending to these effects that animals ensure their own survival. Even a house cat at a dinner party invariably seeks out the person in the room who least likes cats, not to pester him, but as a manner of apology and in a desire for rapprochement. Similarly, whenever Lena experienced an episode of heightened mourning, the chimp Hans Selye offered her chunks of green apple more often, but with the unintended consequence of increasing her misery.

In her grief, Lena was drawn to reading scientific books written by her late husband, volumes that previously hadn't interested her. Now, she entered their pages believing they might in some way revivify him. The activity was without success, however, if success is measured by the alleviation of suffering, for Hans Selye's books possessed a dry, detached tone that lacked the charms and ironies of his private manner. What was worse, she had to admit that his private manner had often been distant and aloof in later years, and the books were reminders of this fact.

It didn't help that the theories expressed in his publications were odious to her. At some level, she already knew them well enough, having endured many receptions and award ceremonies at which she'd heard people praise Hans Selye's work. In those settings, his ideas had been burnished by his growing fame, so that Lena had dwelt on their greatness rather than their implications. Now, reading his magnum opus, *The Stress of Life*, she saw that her husband's view of the universe was repugnantly simplistic, one in which organisms were defined by their susceptibility to irritation. Hans Selye's universe was hostile to humanity, every phenomenon reducible to its chemical excoriations of the brain and body. With horror, she thought back upon her marriage to him and wondered how much time Hans Selye had spent during those forty-two years assessing the quantity of stress she caused him.

Those nights when Lena read her husband's books, the chimp Hans Selye stewed in his cage. He saw the books as dead creatures that she carried about with her, grooming them in a way that was foolish because they never groomed her in return. Lena's inability to recognize the books' failure of reciprocity saddened him; it marked her out as a lesser thing.

Once Hans Selye grew into maturity, Lena was alarmed to discover that he became ever less an adorable little ape and ever more the raucous, foul-smelling animal his mother had been. Worse, Hans flew into rages when he didn't get his way, sometimes biting Lena hard enough to break the skin. She was loath to visit the hospital for fear the authorities would take Hans from her, so she was laid low by infections and long-suppurating wounds that, not having properly been stitched, left fierce scars. Hans's rages terrified and confused her; she still clung to an idea of him that she had developed in his infancy, when he'd been affectionate and biddable. A part of her recognized that she should have given up Hans long ago, but this recognition only made her all the more resolved to keep him, because she hated to admit mistakes.

Lena spent her later years looking for more viable perspectives on the world than the one offered in Hans Selye's books. She took night courses through an extension school and learned about the major religions. She read the *Upali Sutta* and *The Tibetan Book of the Dead*, and she became conversant with the doctrine of reincarnation. Even at this juncture, it never occurred to her that her husband might have been reborn as a chimp. Instead, her mind turned to her own approaching death and what might lie beyond it. *This life is the soil*, she read, *in which the seeds of the next are planted. Some are reborn to the heavens, and some are reborn as hungry ghosts.*

It took over twenty years for her to die. By that time, Hans Selye held no more memory of his simian youth than of his previous life as a famous scientist, or of the life before that as a nuthatch, or of the one before that as a longshoreman, or of any of the previous lives stretching through the millennia. Nor did Hans think forward to his own demise. It was the rising smell of death on Lena that sent him into fits, less potent but wilder than those of his youth. Now Lena kept him locked in his cage at all times so he could inflict harm only upon himself. His incarceration saddened both of them, because she understood his sense of betrayal, and because he didn't understand her guilt. For hours each day, she sat outside the cage just beyond his reach, safe and alien, wishing he would show her a sign of forgiveness, while she bent over books that promised consolation. *Living and dying shall continue*, she read to him, *until ignorance and craving cease. The stream-enterer and the once-returned abandon their fetters.*

It was in this position, seated on the living room floor, that she died the morning of June 21, 2003. By this time, her husband's colleagues and admirers had long ceased to visit, and several days passed before her body was discovered beside the cage of the hysterical, hungry, grieving chimp.

Hans Selye was rusticated to a wildlife sanctuary in the Eastern Townships, where he was billeted in a stable with other refugees – a Shetland pony, a pair of greyhounds, seven peafowl – none of whom had the least notion that the ape in their midst was the reincarnation of the famous scientist Hans Selye. Though they left him in peace, sometimes meditating on the mysteries of their own recurring selves, sometimes merely waiting for dinner, the chimp was never quite at ease in his new surroundings, as the peafowl's cries reminded him of Lena's weeping. If his thoughts on the matter had been only a little more advanced, he might have wondered whether one of those beautiful green birds was the reincarnation of his former wife. But, in fact, Lena had been reborn as a goshawk near the city of Norwich, England, where now she circled and circled above the fens, tracing helices as if shucking off some imperishable excess, searching for creatures in the long grass below, hunting for a satisfaction that promised to be hers if only she looked carefully enough.

THE ISLE OF THANET

When the man at the cathedral gate discovered that Cam was no longer a student, he wouldn't let her in. He said the only other way of gaining admission without paying was to apply for a resident's pass. That would require her to live within four miles of Canterbury, though, and Herne Bay was twice that far. The idea of spending fourteen pounds to visit precincts that she had grown used to wandering for free annoyed her, so she left and headed back on the bus.

Her accent was to blame, she decided. If not for her Canadian vowels, he wouldn't have checked her student card's expiry date.

'The problem's not your voice, my love,' the lifeguard said when Cam stopped on her way home to complain about the man at the cathedral. 'You just had rotten luck.'

She wished the lifeguard wouldn't call her his love, though she knew he meant well. Maybe if he ever patrolled the stretch of shingle beach in front of her hut, she'd try to make friends, but he always parked his van at the other end of Wantsum Walk, and she saw him only when passing by on her way to buy groceries in the village or to refill her water bottles from the sink in the public loo.

When she'd first confessed her living situation to him, he'd seemed amused, no doubt because he couldn't imagine what full-time residence in a beach hut actually involved. The hut had no running water, electricity, or heat. Each morning, she washed herself in the sea. She'd given up meat and dairy; her phone and laptop, too, with their rare-earth metals. She'd stopped buying anything plastic, forsworn kids and pets to lighten the planet's load. To her mother's horror, she also refused to move back home, knowing the carbon cost of a transatlantic flight.

Her mother had sent Cam a letter asking if her decision to stay in Britain was revenge for some perceived slight. Or was it, as Cam's father suspected, the influence of activist professors? What should Cam's parents tell Sean and Seamus and the rest of the extended family? That Cam had been waylaid by a quarter-life crisis?

Cam had replied that the crisis was the whole world's. As long as the glaciers retreated and the rainforests burned, she would strand herself here. She would live patiently with less.

It was late September, drizzling hard. The three weeks she'd been in Herne Bay, there'd been rain every day. This time of year, few people came to the beach – mostly windsurfers in wetsuits. The neon lights at the restaurant had been turned off for the season, and not a soul moved on the pier. The bumper cars sat empty in their pavilion. An old man in a yellow mackintosh criss-crossed the shingles, metal-detecting, and when she smiled at him, he gave her a cold stare. The sky and sea were grey on grey.

She walked the esplanade, counting the wooden groynes set into the beach at intervals of fifty paces, not knowing their purpose. Erosion control maybe, or privacy for hypothetical holi-dayers enjoying the hypothetical sun, or maybe just to satisfy the mania for order on this island where every field had a fence, every forest a name, and every hut in the double row at the espla-nade's far end was a different colour than its neighbours in a way that seemed cheerfully obsessive.

As she reached the first of the huts, a thudding entered her ears from unseen speakers. In the same moment, she saw a man sitting on the porch of a baby-blue hut halfway down the row. It was the hut in front of hers, blocking her view of the sea. The thudding grew louder as she neared him.

'All right?' he called out. A few months ago, she would have taken the phrase to express concern. He sounded local and looked about her age, and he sat in a deck chair, vaping, while a pair of surfboards leaned against the hut. The music came from inside. She said good morning back, but the shudder of the bass annoyed her, so she continued on wordlessly, turning sideways to shuffle through the narrow space between his hut and the next.

In her hut, the sound of the music was only borderline offensive, mostly drowned out by the rain. She let herself hope that he'd lower the volume, now that he knew she was here. He'd seemed friendly enough.

After setting down her bag, she withdrew the morning's acquisitions: canisters for the gas heater, fresh batteries, two bananas, and the paperbacks she'd bought at the charity shop. Then she changed out of her wet clothes and crawled into her sleeping bag with the most promising of the books. She wasn't even through the preface when the music got louder.

Before deciding to rent the hut, she'd worried about noise. Waves and gulls were one thing, music something else. The threat of other people's music, the memory of all the nights she'd been kept up by it at university back home, was the main reason she'd rented her own flat after arriving in Canterbury, even though she couldn't afford it; even though the student residence would have let her get to know people, would have helped her to adapt more quickly to England, wouldn't have made her so lonely and susceptible to the first plummy chat-up line she heard. Now that she thought of it, she'd been putting the blame in the wrong place. It was music that had ruined her life, the fear of music like what was playing now and stopping her from reading, when reading was the only thing in the world for her to do.

She bore down on the page in front of her, trying to gain traction with the sentence she was on, taking runs at it like a driver tackling a too-steep driveway in the snow.

Perhaps every dragon in our lives is a princess waiting –
Perhaps every dragon in our lives is in our lives –
Perhaps every dragon is a princess in our lives –

She threw the book against the wall. Then she slid out of her sleeping bag and pulled on her rain shell, trying not to get worked up by anticipating an argument. Better to think that he'd cranked the volume because he didn't realize she was next door. Maybe he was lonely, just needed to hear someone else's voice, even a recorded one, to distract him from his own thoughts.

When she knocked, the door of his hut stood ajar, leaking pulses of electropop, the same four bars over and over.

'And here I thought you weren't going to speak to me,' he said, opening the door wider. 'Come on in.'

She hesitated.

'I promise not to murder you,' he said.

The hut was the same size as hers but seemed smaller because of the clutter. A wooden pole running horizontally along one wall had been draped with wetsuits, towels, and coils of rope. An unmade cot lay in the corner. A folding table held a few bottles of alcohol, a stack of plastic cups, and an old-school boombox. Resisting the urge to go over and turn it off, she pivoted to round out her survey of the room. Then she jumped. In the nearest corner sat a woman in an armchair, staring at her. She looked barely out of her teens, with short black hair, wearing a wetsuit that was unzipped to her collarbone.

Cam had got it wrong then. The guy wasn't some solitary sad sack.

He said something, and Cam cupped a hand to her ear to show she couldn't hear him. He went to the boombox but only turned it down a little, so that he was still practically shouting when he said they were Aidan and Becky, from the Isle of Thanet.

Cam told them her name and that she was from Canada, thinking it might count for something that she wasn't from the States.

'What are you doing here?' Becky asked. There was no welcome in her tone.

'Just hoping you might turn off the music,' Cam said.

Becky smirked, and Cam realized she'd misunderstood the question. She considered making another stab at a reply, but it was too late. A look passed between Aidan and Becky.

'The walls are super thin,' Cam said. 'It's hard for me to concentrate.'

'That's terrible,' said Aidan. 'I mean, really awful.'

She felt herself flush and decided to try making a joke of it. 'First-world problems, right?'

'I'm so sorry we've been hurting your *concentration*,' Aidan said.

Becky stared at the floorboards with pursed lips.

'You don't need to turn the music all the way off,' Cam found herself saying. 'You could just turn it down.' The nearest café was a mile away in the rain. It closed at four. She had nowhere else to go.

'We'd love to turn it down, but you know what?' Aidan waited as if expecting a reply.

Cam decided to appeal again to Becky. 'Would you mind? Please?'

'It's a beach,' said Aidan. 'You don't come to a beach to concentrate.'

Becky finally raised her eyes. She gave Cam a pitying look. 'He's right. You have to expect some noise.'

The hut had grown too hot. Cam needed to get out of there. 'Will you just tell me – ' she said, then stopped to take a breath. 'How long are you going to be here?'

'The rest of the day,' said Aidan with a grin.

'Will you be back after that?' said Cam.

He nodded. 'Every day this week, probably.'

She decided to give Becky another try. 'I go out of the hut a few times a day. I can let you know when I leave, and you can play music then.' As long as it was her speaking, she could maintain the illusion that the three of them were having a reasonable conversation.

'Sorry, darling, it's the beach,' said Aidan.

'Okay, thanks,' said Cam, as if he'd told her something else. She left without saying goodbye.

Once she was back in her hut, the music grew even louder, then cut out. She waited, not wanting to get her hopes up, before returning to her sleeping bag.

'Darling,' she muttered. 'Darling.'

A few minutes later, she heard them yelling at each other. She couldn't make out the words.

Rain or no rain, she had to go somewhere. It occurred to her that there could be noise at the café, too, so she headed out in the other direction, all the way to the end of the esplanade, before following the cliff-edge path toward the Roman fort. Below her sat a catamaran pulled up on shore with weeds sprouting between the pontoons. The rigging banged against the mast like a slow clap. When she returned to the huts, Aidan and Becky's was shut up tight, giving no sign that anyone had been there.

If granted a second chance, she decided, she'd offer Becky a friendly warning. Don't you see what kind of person he is? You're so young. You can't let someone like that take advantage of you, or they'll make your life a disaster.

The next day at noon, the rain and music started up together. Cam had just finished a lunch of baked beans straight from the tin, sopping up the sauce with a heel of bread. The music was the first human sound she'd heard all day. It was noxious synthetic noise, no different from methane or carbon monoxide: one more toxic by-product of human selfishness. She got ready for another walk.

When she stepped outside, the music still played, and she could see two people in the surf. One was Aidan, skimming the waves on a kite board, tethered to a little puffed-out parachute. The other was Becky, lying belly-down on a surfboard. Out there, they wouldn't hear the music. Their hut's door wasn't even open. Cam knocked and got no answer. Aidan must have left the boombox going just to make her miserable. She'd switch it off. If they came to accuse her, she'd confess freely.

Gripping the door handle, she yanked and found it locked.

The rain came down harder. She dragged out the walk as long as she could before the weather defeated her. When she returned, they were still out there, the music still blaring. In her hut, she set water to boil on the camp stove. It was Sunday, which meant the café was closed, and the council office, too. Tomorrow, she'd find out about the noise bylaws, except she didn't know how to file a complaint without drawing attention to the fact that she was living in a beach hut, which was, in all likelihood, more illegal than playing music. Her only other option was to confront them again, and the thought made her sick. Aidan could go to hell.

Becky, though; Cam wanted to believe that she could get through to Becky. She reached under her mattress for her notepad and began to write.

Dear Becky,
Would you come see me? I'd be grateful if you would.
                                                                    Cam

She dashed to their hut, rifled the note under the door, then ran back and dove for her sleeping bag. She lay there trying to make out her heartbeat but hearing only the thud of the bass. When it finally ended, she was too tired to be relieved.

The rain still hadn't stopped when a sound from outside woke her. A shadow flickered in the space between the door and its frame. A piece of paper had been slid through the crack: a flyer for the Chaucer festival, with writing scribbled in pencil on the other side.

> *Sorry how Aidan acted yesterday. I'll try to keep him from playing his music.*
>
> *– Becky*
>
> *PS – I think the songs he likes are pants. (That means crap.)*

Cam smiled. It was the closest to happiness she'd felt in weeks.

The next morning, she read distractedly, wanting it to be eleven-thirty, time for her weekly check-in with Stef. The meetings were Stef's idea. She said they were to let her keep enjoying Cam's company, now that they no longer had classes together, but probably she worried about Cam drowning herself in the sea. Cam had agreed to the meetings because Stef was willing to make the trip from Canterbury, and because Stef had promised to avoid a list of topics earmarked by Cam as taboo. They included the past year and Cam's future, as well as anything to do with the Literature department in which they had both been students and of which Stef was still a member.

Cam set out early to stop at the post office on the way and see if the twins had written her. Since she'd moved into the hut, the only word of them she'd received had been in her mother's letters. Before that, back when Cam had a phone, Seamus and Sean had replied to her texts faithfully, but even then, their messages always carried the whiff of younger relatives humouring an elder. Cam couldn't expect more; the twins were busy teenagers with sports and video games and part-time jobs to occupy them, and she hadn't lived with them for years. Now, they were off to university, far from home themselves. They had better things to do than write her.

There was nothing for her at the post office, not even from her mother, who wrote practically every other day, and Cam arrived at the café half an hour early. Stef got there ten minutes late, carrying a plastic bag with a shoebox poking out of it. When she sat down at the table, she deposited the box at her feet and gave Cam a once-over, as she'd done all month by way of greeting, searching for actionable signs of self-neglect. Cam wanted to protest, but their lunch together might be the only proper human interaction she got all week. She didn't like the look of the box, though.

'What's in that?' she said.

'Oh – I was saving it for later.'

From the way Stef spoke, Cam knew who it was from. 'You told her I'm here, didn't you?'

'No, I swear. All I said was that I see you sometimes. Whenever I run into her, she asks after you.'

'You promised not to tell her anything.'

'Well, I'm sorry. She's worried about how you're doing. I think she wishes that you'd continued on with doctoral studies, too.'

Cam made a face. 'No, she's glad I'm gone. If I were still there, she'd be afraid of me telling everybody about her and me.'

'You wouldn't, would you?' Stef sounded partial to the possibility.

'No. It would look like sour grapes.' A choice had been made, and Cam hadn't been chosen. It was as simple as that.

'Anyhow, I checked, and it's allowed,' said Stef. 'I mean, you must know this already, but the university rules say it's okay as long as the professor isn't grading you.' Her voice held a note of doubt; it probably hadn't escaped her attention that when Cam had told her the whole story, she'd been hazy about the timeline.

They sat in silence for a while. Then Cam nodded toward the box, and Stef handed it over. When Cam lifted the top, she found four books inside with an envelope lying on top of them. She opened it and pulled out a note written in a familiar scrawl.

My dear C,

I attempted to pare down my library, as per yr decluttering suggestion in July, & thought these might be useful for yr research. The Storr, esp. Dated now, & chauvinist, but his ideas re: the rel. b/n solitude & a ~~maternal~~ – ahem, <u>parental</u> – presence could be grist to yr mill.

Hard for me to let go of books. Easier if I imagine these w/ you.

w/ fondness, Aldie

If Cam had been on her own, she would have crumpled the note there and then.

'What does it say?' said Stef.

'Nothing. Practically nothing.' Cam shoved it back into the envelope.

'I guess that's good? I worried she'd get your hopes up.'

Cam's heart panged. 'No, it's over. I told you, she was pretty definitive.' She jammed the envelope into her backpack, then pushed the shoebox across the table. 'Take it. I don't want more stuff.' She shouldn't have bullshitted Aldie about going on a research trip. She'd done it only because she figured that if Aldie knew her real plan, she'd accuse her of being dramatic. Research, in contrast, was like breathing to Aldie: necessary and unquestionable.

Without asking, Stef opened the box to examine the books. 'You think she meant these as a peace offering? Maybe she feels bad about what happened – '

'She feels fine. She got what she wanted. Rescued from her mid-life crisis by some young blood.'

Stef's brow knitted a little. She turned toward the plate-glass window facing the street. 'Have you thought about what you're doing out here? I mean, I get that it's for the planet. But maybe, at some level – are you waiting for her? Staying close in case she changes her mind?'

Cam grimaced. 'You want to talk about my mommy issues, too?'

Stef winced, and Cam realized her mistake. Stef's mother had died in the spring. Cam didn't know how to apologize without making things worse.

'Stef – ' she began.

'Forget it,' said Stef. 'Let's talk about something else.'

Almost home, Cam saw Aidan and Becky out on their boards again. Her gut clenched, but as she drew closer, the only sounds were of the waves against the shore.

In her hut, she reread Aldie's note. '*Hard for me to let go of books.*' Whenever Aldie spoke or wrote, she chose each word fastidiously. For that reason alone, Cam's time with her had been intimidating. Aldie worked on too many levels at once. Once the relationship ended, all those levels had constituted another reason for Cam to get away. She didn't want to hang around the department parsing Aldie's every phrase.

Dinner that night was instant noodles, a handful of almonds, and an unpeeled carrot. When Cam went to rinse her plate in the sea, the sun had set, and the surfboards leaned against Aidan and Becky's hut. Their door was shut, light streaming out from the cracks. Surely they weren't going to stay over. Only Cam was crazy enough to do that. They had a cot, though. A few months ago, the idea of a night on the beach with your lover would have excited her. Now, she returned to her hut and got out the flashlight to read.

A moment later, the music started.

It wasn't right. She had to tell them to shut up. Maybe it would be easier now that she knew she had Becky on her side. Except if that was true, why was the music playing?

Then an answer came to her. At night, the music might not be bullying. It might be masking noises she didn't want to hear. A neighbour's courtesy.

The thought was too much. She decided to go bathing. It was dark out, but she didn't care. She got into her swimsuit, took her flashlight and her biodegradable soap, and stepped into the night. When she went by Aidan and Becky's hut, the music's loudness so enraged her that, despite herself, she slapped her palm against the wall. She hoped for a shout of protest from within, for Aidan to throw open the door so she could yell at him, but he didn't appear.

When she reached the shingles, the music stopped. The wind had picked up, and tall waves broke on the shore. She considered turning back, but she'd made a decision. She wasn't going to put herself at the mercy of other people's whims.

In the water, the stones underfoot were slick and loose. She fell and lost a sandal, thrashed about trying to find it, had no luck. It didn't matter; the thing would wash up on its own. She began to scrub herself with the soap, so that she didn't notice the beam from the flashlight until it was halfway between the huts and the water, moving toward her.

'What are you doing?' said a voice. It was Aidan. Through the darkness, she could see Becky standing next to him. Cam tried to stay upright as the waves crashed into her. The flashlight's beam slid onto her body. She threw her arms around herself and squinted until the beam whipped back onto land.

'I'm bathing,' she shouted. 'Give me some privacy.'

'You just bashed our hut, didn't you?' he said. 'You seem to want attention, not privacy.'

Becky reached for his arm and spoke to him, too softly for Cam to hear.

'I'm not drunk!' he shouted, shrugging her off. Returning his attention to Cam, he said, 'Are you looking for company? We can make it a party.'

She didn't reply.

'Come back to shore,' he said. 'You can't stand there in those waves. It's dangerous.'

If Becky had been the one to say it, Cam would have obliged her. 'Go away,' she said instead. 'I'll get out when you're gone.'

He set the flashlight on the ground so that it stayed pointing at her, then stepped into the water, arms spread wide for balance. He wore nothing but a pair of boxer shorts. Feeling ill at the thought of him touching her, she began to swim away from the shore, following the lights of a freighter on the horizon.

Behind her, Becky called for him to stop, then started screaming his name. Cam entertained a thought that made her turn.

She couldn't see him anywhere. Becky had waded in up to her knees but seemed fearful of going farther. Finally, Cam spotted him struggling in the water, not far from the shore. She swore and swam back, muscles aching from the cold, every wave carrying her as far as several strokes.

One morning in mid-August, Cam had knocked on the front door of Aldie's house, despite having been told at the last minute not to come. It was a reckless thing to do, but Aldie had teased her all week about her husband's trip to London, about having the place to herself, and it wasn't like she and Cam hadn't been reckless before, not just in the house but in various locations, from Aldie's office to the woods near the university.

Aldie wasn't the one who answered. The husband did. Cam had never met him, but she knew his face from photographs around the house. She stammered a hello and asked if Professor Richardson was home.

'I'm afraid she's not feeling well,' the husband said. 'May I tell her who called?'

Cam froze and said nothing. He took her in with sad eyes.

'Are you one of her students?' he prompted gently.

Cam's head began to throb. He knew. From the way he'd spoken, she was certain he did. She wanted to turn and run, but some mechanism in her insisted on keeping up appearances, so she nodded.

'Do you have an essay to give her?' he asked with the hint of a smile.

'Students drop off essays here?' she replied. The idea seemed incredible: the house was a half-hour walk from the campus.

'No, never,' he said. The hint of smile vanished. 'But once, someone else in your position pretended to be here for that.'

Cam heard in his voice a certainty that he'd outlast her. That his kind of fidelity had more dignity than hers.

'Are you all right?' he said. 'You look ill. Would you like to come in and sit down?'

Cam shook her head, fixing her gaze on the welcome mat. He said goodbye and stepped back to close the door.

She walked home clutching her phone, desperate to talk with Aldie, to beg her forgiveness for the intrusion. But she'd been told never to ring or text, and it seemed best not to make things worse by violating the instruction. As it turned out, she had to wait until the next day before Aldie called to end things.

It felt like a long time, but probably wasn't, before Aidan rolled over and vomited up a stream of sea water, then returned to lying on his back, coughing and panting. Cam told him to hold still. He had to trust her on this, she'd taken a CPR course, and it was dangerous for him to move; he needed to stay as he was until help arrived.

'I'm sorry this happened,' she told Becky once the paramedics turned up. Becky's face was buried in her phone, thumbs twitching out a message. It struck Cam that this would be the last time they ever saw each other.

'Listen, I wanted to say thank you,' Cam said.

Becky's nose wrinkled. 'For what?'

'For your note. It meant a lot to me.'

Becky scowled. 'That was just Aidan and me taking the piss.'

One of the paramedics told Cam that she'd saved that man's life. He said that if she stuck around, the council might give her a medal. Then he offered her a lift home. She said that she'd be fine.

'What will you do next?' the lifeguard asked in the morning, after she described the night's events. He was keeping an eye on a little girl near the surf who was digging in the shingles with a plastic shovel, while a woman in a long coat paced the esplanade, studying the pavement, as if she'd forgotten that she and the girl were together.

Cam said she thought her time in the hut was up. She'd been imagining travel. Had he ever heard of the Isle of Thanet? She liked the name; it sounded exotic.

'You mean over there?' he said, pointing. When she frowned, he explained that the Isle of Thanet was the tip of Kent, a few miles east. It hadn't been an actual island for a long time, but with the sea level rising nowadays, you never knew.

'I didn't realize,' she said. 'I thought it was somewhere else.'

She looked at her watch. There'd be a bus to Canterbury in an hour. If she hurried, she could make it. From there, a train to London. And then? Last year, there'd been so much going on that she hadn't seen any of the country, much less places beyond. She'd buy a Eurail pass. She'd get a bicycle. She'd tell Stef that she was leaving but not where she was headed, because she didn't know.

On the beach, the little girl ran across the shingles toward the pacing woman. The girl was shouting in jubilation, but whatever she said, the wind smothered it, offering only the sting of grit from the mud flats darkly distant, flung again and again onto the esplanade with the rotten-egg smell of the sea.

APRICOTS

Once the bus finally started to move, I got a craving for unsulphured apricots. A bunch of kids had just sat down around us, and I was pissed off about it. They were that loud-mouthed age where the girls are wearing crop tops and the boys are sneaking glances at the girls' bodies between swearing and smacking each other. I could never stand apricots, but when Ruthie was pregnant I bought loads of them for her, and when she moved on to pickles and creamed corn, all of a sudden there we were with an empty bank account and twelve pounds of unsulphured apricots from the health food co-operative, and Ruthie said how she would throw up if she ever had to eat another one. Maybe the baby would like them, I suggested. No, they'll go bad, she said. Chuck them. So I opened a bag and decided they tasted better than shoe leather, which was what we'd be eating by the time the little beggar finally arrived, the way things were going. I went through all twelve pounds in two weeks and had a bout of diarrhea that almost ended the marriage. Sitting on that bus, I thought how it had been months since I'd eaten an unsulphured apricot.

The baby was trying to bite Ruthie again. I said we were going to have to buy a muzzle. He wasn't a baby anymore, although sometimes I accused him of it: *Only babies act like that. Stop acting like a baby.* Ruthie told me not to be silly. He's two, he doesn't understand. I said oh, he knows what I mean, and I stared at him hard, which got him howling all over again.

The little guy wouldn't even come near me when he was upset. I'd go to pick him up if he'd bumped his head, and it didn't matter if he'd given himself a concussion, he had this fail-safe guidance system that sent him running for his mother. Usually I took it okay. It was just once that it got to me.

'Aren't I his father?' I yelled that time. 'I mean, what the hell?' I was close to crying, which is the one thing I never should have started to do in front of Ruthie. It used to feel okay, but lately it's been more and more like I'm surrendering something. 'I mean, did you go to a sperm bank or what?' I tried to say it as a joke.

'Is this about sex, Peter?' she wanted to know. We hadn't had it for weeks.

'Oh, come on,' I said, which was as close to a confession as she was going to get.

The bus climbed a ramp off the city street onto the highway, and the baby stopped trying to bite her and started ripping at her hair, and for the first time I noticed that the kids in the seats across from us had a package of apricots, the sulphured kind that are radioactive orange. They weren't eating them, they were just squishing them in their fingers and throwing them at each other. I figured I must have already seen the apricots out of the corner of my eye, and that glimpse had started the craving.

I watched an apricot go halfway up the bus. A little harder, I thought, and it would have hit the driver. Then he'd pull over and kick the brats out. I cheered for each flying apricot to make it to the front and bounce off that cap of his, until one of them took a wrong turn off the top of a seat and hit me in the nose.

I think that a proper man wouldn't have minded what happened next to the apricot. He would have just turned to stare at the kids, and that would have put an end to everything. But instead, the first thing I did was start looking for the one that had nailed me, patting down my jacket and pawing the floor with my foot. Maybe I thought I'd earned the right to throw it back at them, or maybe I really was that hungry for apricots, and

I thought I could salvage it and scarf it down right there. But all of my rummaging just got them interested, like they'd spotted an endangered species. They were talking in a foreign language, Swedish or something, and getting excited.

'You idiots,' I said loudly, then frowned at myself. That wasn't the right phrase for an adult. I hoped they didn't know much English. 'Sit back and behave yourselves.'

Ruthie cooed to the baby, who was still thrashing and moaning a little. The Swedish kids looked at each other; then they grinned and got comfortable. Their seat was staggered a bit behind ours, and when I turned, I realized that this position gave them an advantage: they could just sit there and watch me, out of sight. I started scrolling the news on my phone and tried not to think about them. But I heard whispering, the shifting of bodies, and I could feel their beady little eyes fixing on the side of my face. Ruthie had better keep him from screaming, I thought, or I'm going to snap.

Then an apricot hit my shoulder and went tumbling into the aisle. Some reflex started turning me around for a confrontation, but I told myself it was just what they wanted, so I jerked to a standstill, and I thought how it probably looked twice as hilarious to them, me turning halfway like that. I shook my head, and that felt like a better gesture of disapproval – as though I was above anything they could do to me. It was all the reaction I was going to allow myself anymore.

The next apricot got me right in the ear and fell into Ruthie's hair.

'You assholes,' I shouted, standing up. 'We have a little kid here, don't you see that? You want one of those things to hit him and knock out his eye? Grow the fuck up.' I turned and saw the driver watching me in the rear-view mirror. Good, I thought, let him stop the bus. I sat down and he didn't do anything, but there had been enough beats in the silence after my voice for the baby to start screaming. They never do it right away, they give you a few beats to fill up with dread.

'There, see what you did?' I said to the kids. 'That's your fault. Hope you like it.'

Ruthie was really quiet now, holding the baby so patiently, and I remembered how it had been a long morning of tantrums and how she'd already been at her wit's end in the motel room. I wanted to stroke her hair, but I ended up just picking out the apricot, wrapping it in Kleenex, and putting it in my pocket.

He wouldn't stop crying. When I turned around again a few minutes later, even the Swedish kids looked annoyed. They stared and scowled and made comments to one another. I scowled back. Look at her, I thought; she doesn't even notice any of it. She's in this bubble of her and the baby.

This was all half an hour in. It was a four-hour trip, mostly on highways, and eventually the thrum of the engine took hold of people and calmed them down. Everyone but me was sleeping. My face had cooled off, and I was thinking about how once we got to my parents', we could ask them to look after him for a while. Then we could have some time to ourselves for once. I looked from Ruthie to the baby, and from the baby to those Swedish kids nestled against each other and their eyelids flickering with dreams, and it still wasn't clear to me whether you're born with an ability to love your fellow human beings, or whether it's something that keeps ballooning and shrivelling all the way along.

KNOCK, KNOCK

The two of them were checking out the only decently sized bedroom in the place when Meleka's phone rang.

'Don't answer this time,' Jacob said. 'Can't the kid manage five minutes on his own?'

He heard her say hello just before she closed the door of the en suite, sealing herself inside. He would have lingered to see if he could hear anything, but another couple entered the bedroom, each with a printout of the listing in hand, so he stepped into the hallway.

Jacob and Meleka's agent had been surprised when Jacob told him they preferred open houses to private viewings. Nobody who has a choice prefers open houses, the agent said. People like having a place to themselves. Jacob had refrained from pointing out that open houses were simpler because they let him and Meleka look at properties without the agent's constant yapping. Jacob had also refrained from saying how open houses gave him the chance, if he saw something small that he liked, a fountain pen or soapstone carving or some other tchotchke, to slip it into his pocket.

Meleka knew about the habit because Jacob had told her. When he'd confessed, she'd said it wasn't for her to judge, but she did warn him about nanny cams. Then he'd asked what she thought it meant that he went around taking people's stuff.

'That's not my job anymore,' she'd replied.

'I'm not looking for your professional opinion,' he'd said. 'Just what you think.'

She'd given a long sigh. 'Okay, I reckon it's because you don't really want a new house, and you're trying to sabotage the process, hoping you get caught.'

'How can you say that?' he'd protested. 'Haven't you seen the checklist on my phone?'

He'd tried to make it sound like he was kidding, but he wasn't. He'd got the checklist off a website. At open houses, it helped him keep an eye out for details you wouldn't catch in photos. Houses were so diabolically staged that it was easy to be taken in, to forget there could be knob-and-tube, ceiling stains, uninsulated walls.

At his mention of the checklist, Meleka had only shrugged. 'The checklist helps you find excuses not to make an offer,' she'd said.

Now, he went along to the smallest bedroom, which was evidently serving as an office, not just staged as one, because it had a boxy old computer and flatbed scanner sitting on a cheap IKEA desk that nobody would put there for looks. Finding the room empty, Jacob started opening the desk drawers. The top one was crammed with office supplies. The middle one held a bottle of whisky too big for his pocket. In the bottom drawer, tucked in beside a sheaf of folders, lay a knife, four inches long, the blade folded into a cream-coloured handle. Elephant ivory; maybe mammoth. Not as rare as it used to be, now that the permafrost in Siberia was melting, but still impressive.

He couldn't believe some people. It was as if they didn't think anyone would open their medicine cabinets or snoop in their closets. He'd found Rolexes, sex toys, Percocet, hash. You could take anything from bathrooms, because nobody would admit to installing a nanny cam there, and with contraband you had carte blanche, because they wouldn't tell the cops. Of course, the homeowners themselves might come after you. The trick was to sign the register with a fake name.

He pocketed the knife, then stepped out of the room to see Meleka heading his way.

'We have to go home,' she said.

'Why?' he asked, knowing the answer. She capitulated to the kid's demands in a way that she never did with any of her other clients. He wasn't even a kid either; he was a grown-ass man.

'He's having one of his anxiety attacks,' Meleka said. 'I told him we could meet.'

'The cops still haven't arrested him?'

'If they had, he wouldn't be able to meet, would he?'

Once they'd left, the knife in Jacob's pocket cried to be exhibited, but he held off. It still amazed him that he could just take things. He'd never stolen anything in his life until he and Meleka started looking at houses. Maybe he missed their sessions and still needed to confess things to her. Whatever the reason, she'd done little to discourage him. The first time, when he'd shown her the thumb drive that he'd smuggled out of the split-level on Hawthorn, she'd only laughed and asked if he wanted her to tell him he was naughty.

He hadn't dared to check the drive for files. At first, he'd left it sitting on their nightstand. Then, in a moment of paranoia, he'd carried it to the basement and smashed it with the club hammer from his mother's toolbox. It took three swings before the plastic cracked.

The latest open house had brought them across town to a neighbourhood dominated by postwar bungalows. The area was a long way from hip, but they couldn't be choosy if they wanted a detached place. All they had was his mother's life insurance payout, whatever they'd get for the townhouse, and a small, grudging sum from Meleka's parents, who, judging by their demeanour on Zoom, still hoped their daughter's Stockholm syndrome would wear off and she'd return to Australia.

The weather was weirdly warm, May-like, though still mid-March, with dirty snow piles at the ends of driveways furiously shedding water. As the two of them went along the sidewalk toward the car, he wanted to hold her hand, but it clutched her balled-up jacket.

'You're worried about the kid?' he said.

'Yeah.'

'He'll be all right. You're doing a great job with him.'

He tried to think up a joke for her. Improvised ones were his specialty. Most often, knock-knock jokes. The first time he'd tried one on her, mid-session, she'd laughed like he'd discovered a cheat code rendering her attraction to him suddenly possible. Now, it took him a minute to come up with something.

'Knock, knock,' he said finally.

She smiled a bit. 'Who's there?'

'I wuv woo.'

She seemed doubtful. 'I wuv woo who?'

'Aw, I'm so glad it's mutual!'

She laughed, but not very convincingly.

At the car, they didn't argue over who would drive as they often had upon first arriving in the country together. Six months ago, her Australian licence had expired, and she still hadn't applied for a Canadian one. She'd need to take a road test now. It was probably his fault that she'd waited; if he'd found a job, he wouldn't always be there to give her rides.

'You think the kid's panicking because he's guilty?' Jacob asked on the drive home. The kid's name was Devin, but Meleka never called him that, so Jacob didn't either. He knew the name only because he'd peeked in her files.

'He's innocent,' she said. 'Four sessions a week, you get a good idea. He has issues with boundaries, but he's harmless.'

'The cops seem to disagree.'

'They haven't arrested him.'

'But they think he's their guy.'

She wouldn't have talked to the cops if the kid hadn't sent them, thinking it would reassure the authorities to hear from his counsellor – his therapist, really, but Meleka couldn't call herself one now. Therapists had to observe a five-year waiting period before they could sleep with a former patient. In Australia, she and Jacob had come up short by four years and eleven months.

Jacob knew things were hard for her. So far, she had four clients. Her family and friends were all on the other side of the world. At least she was young enough not to have built up much of a client base there. At least nobody in her professional life had found out about the two of them. Still, she'd said that a move overseas might head off trouble.

The drive home took twenty minutes. They'd just turned onto their street when she told him to pull over.

'Damn it,' she said. 'He's already there.'

Jacob pulled over and peered at the townhouse. He'd never seen the kid before and was eager to get a glimpse of him. As it turned out, the guy smoking a cigarette on their doorstep didn't look like a kid at all. He was tall and lanky, with dark hair to his shoulders and a chunky beard. He wore jeans and a white T-shirt, and his arms were covered in tattoos. Instantly, Jacob hated him. Except no, it wasn't quite true; he'd hated him already.

'What should we do?' Jacob said. Meleka had made it clear that under no circumstances could he allow himself to be spotted by clients. They couldn't know that Meleka had a husband; they needed to see her as a blank slate. The problem was that she held her sessions in the living room, which had a wide, doorless opening into the front hallway, rendering visible anyone who passed by on the way outside or upstairs, so that whenever Meleka was in there with someone, Jacob was left trapped upstairs or in the kitchen.

'I'll walk from here,' she told him now. 'Wait until we're inside, then go in the back.'

He watched her leave the car and make her way down the sidewalk. When she reached the townhouse, the kid stamped out his cigarette and grinned. Jacob didn't like how little he moved aside to let her unlock the door. Jacob knew about transference. Counter-transference, too. The kid called her way too often.

With Jacob, it was Meleka who'd made the first move. She'd told him that he'd improved enough for them to end their sessions. Then she'd waited for him to pay his final bill before calling to invite him out. He'd thought she was joking; during their sessions, she'd always been agonizingly professional. When she finally convinced him that the invitation was genuine, he insisted on having her over, cooking a five-course dinner that his mother had taught him to make in case he ever needed to impress people: gazpacho and creviche, tacos and chicken enchiladas. He cheated on the churros, buying them from the bakery down the street, admitting it after Meleka said he'd saved the best for last. Ever since that night, he'd continued to do all the cooking, planning the meals and buying the ingredients. Sometimes, she volunteered to be his sous-chef, chopping vegetables while he told her where he'd found the recipe and why he thought she'd enjoy it. He did the laundry, too, and swept and vacuumed. He cleaned the bathroom twice a week. She said she'd never been cared for like he cared for her.

In Australia, she hadn't told him of the five-year rule until he'd started panicking about his imminent return home once his visa ended. By that point, they'd been sleeping together for two months. A week later, they got married at the registry office with a couple of her friends as witnesses. Jacob couldn't remember their names, only the looks he'd caught them giving each other.

Meleka always swore to him that she'd told the truth about his readiness to end the treatment. These avowals made him worry, because they implied that his ability to keep it together had been a precondition of their relationship. What would happen the next time he cracked up? He'd seen two therapists in high school; two more at university. His mother was the one who'd insisted that he could handle graduate studies overseas. By that point, she'd reached stage four, and he knew that looking after both herself and him had grown too much for her. She died the day before the offer letter came. In Australia, he got through two weeks of classes before heading to the student clinic.

Once Meleka and the kid were inside, Jacob exited the car and walked around the block, down the laneway behind the row of townhouses, to enter through the back door. Then he went to the dining room, still filled with boxes of his mother's things, and placed his ear against the wall shared with the living room. A while ago, he'd figured out that if a client spoke clearly enough, you could hear most of what they said. With Meleka, it was trickier; she always sat facing the street in a velvet armchair she'd shipped from home, and she kept her voice low.

Usually, the kid was loud. Jacob had heard some messed-up things, especially about relationships with exes. Today, he couldn't make out a word. Meleka had once told him of sessions where the hour passed without her or the client uttering a sentence. Jacob tried to picture her and the kid just sitting there, but his brain wouldn't let him. It sent the two of them kaleidoscoping through positions on his mother's couch.

His bladder suddenly felt full. The only bathroom was upstairs. If he went there now, Meleka would be furious. Better to drive to the nearest coffee shop. There was no way he'd make it, though.

Starting up the hallway, he heard their voices. When he passed the living room, the speaking stopped. Turning to climb the stairs, he snuck a glimpse. The kid was sitting on the couch, staring at him, while Meleka glared from her armchair. Jacob quickened his steps.

Upstairs, he stopped at the linen closet to remove the knife from his pocket and slip it under a stack of towels. In the bathroom, he made sure to flush, knowing she'd hear. Then he lay down in their bedroom. He couldn't go back downstairs, not after that look from her. But he'd left his laptop in the kitchen, and his phone didn't have data, because he didn't want to live in thrall to a device.

Surveying the room, he regretted having taken down all his posters, though he'd done it with good intentions, wanting the space to be Meleka's, too, not just his, and hoping it would feel bigger with bare walls. When he was a teenager, he'd fantasized about sharing this room with somebody, if only for an hour or two, but he'd never pulled it off. Sharing it with someone full-time turned out to be another thing entirely. He'd suggested that they move into his mother's room, but Meleka had made a face, so they'd squished their clothes into his closet and bought a tiny nightstand for Meleka's side of the bed. It held the copy of *Anna Karenina* that she'd brought from Australia and still hadn't read. He picked it up and flipped it open.

Twenty pages in, Meleka's voice startled him.

'What the hell were you doing?'

She stood in the doorway, hands on hips.

'Sorry,' he said. 'I needed the bathroom.'

'Now he thinks he's being watched.' There was a pique in her voice he'd never heard before. 'The one thing I needed was quiet. I look after people with problems. I see them for a limited time – '

His face grew hot. 'You talk with him every day – '

' – a limited time, and I can't look after them properly if I'm also having to deal with you.'

She turned to head back down the hallway.

'Where are you going?' he asked.

'I don't know,' she said, hesitating, her voice suddenly doleful. 'I'm trapped here, aren't I? I can't even drive.'

He hurried over to hold her. Her arms stayed hanging at her sides. Reluctantly, he let her go.

'How's the kid doing?' he asked.

'He's a mess. The police are asking him about other assaults. Cases from last year.'

'You still think he's innocent?'

She nodded. Jacob thought again of the kid's grin on the front step.

'You think maybe he's fallen for you?' he said.

Her shoulders slumped. 'May I go type my notes, please?'

He felt his jaw clench. His dentist had told him there was evidence of grinding. After watching her retreat downstairs, he returned to *Anna Karenina*.

By six, his stomach was growling and Meleka hadn't come back upstairs. He found her in her armchair, writing out something on her phone.

'How does fettuccine sound for tonight?' he said.

She nodded without meeting his eyes. 'Is it all right if I don't help? I have to talk with my parents.'

'Sure,' he said, trying not to make a face. 'Hey, before you do: knock, knock.'

Her forehead creased. 'Maybe not now?'

'Come on, you'll like this one.' He'd practised it a few times to get it down properly.

'Fine. Who's there?'

'Palindrome.'

'Palindrome who?'

'Palindrome, palindrome, there who's, knock, knock.'

Her expression didn't change. 'It's clever,' she said.

In the kitchen, he made the pasta and a salad. When he went to check on her, she waved him away, the phone tucked under her chin. He returned to the kitchen and ate alone. Finally, she appeared in the doorway to say that her stomach hurt too much for food. He asked if she wanted a hot-water bottle. Before she could answer, her phone rang. It was the kid. Jacob could tell from her swiftness in heading for the living room as she answered.

He tipped the fettuccine into Tupperware and spent the next half-hour going through real estate listings on his laptop. In bed, he let the YouTube algorithm feed him videos until he fell asleep. When he awoke, it was morning. Rain pattered on the roof. He saw no sign that she'd come upstairs. In the living room, he found her asleep on the couch, still in her clothes, curled under the patchwork quilt that his mother had made between treatments.

On Mondays, Meleka didn't have clients until four. When she woke up, he would ask if the two of them could spend some time together. Watch a movie in bed maybe. They'd done that all the time in Australia, lavishing whole afternoons on each other. He could go to the library now and pick out a DVD. She preferred discs to streaming, said Netflix didn't feel real. If he hurried, he'd be back before she woke.

The branch's selection was small, mostly documentaries and superhero junk. He was about to ask the librarian if anything had been recently returned when their real estate agent called. The screen on Jacob's phone offered a reminder that the guy's name was Tom. Jacob hurried to a quiet corner.

'What did you think of the place on Cranbrook?' Tom wanted to know.

'It was okay,' Jacob replied, suddenly uneasy. They hadn't told him they were going to see it.

'Uh-huh. The listing agent just wrote all the agents in town. A fancy knife went missing at the open house.'

Jacob's heart began to thud. 'Sorry to hear that,' he said.

'The handle's made from a woolly mammoth tusk. Can you believe that? I thought those things were only in museums.'

'Well, I hope they get it back.'

'Mm-hmm,' said Tom, and Jacob knew he was screwed. 'They had a nanny cam in the room. The agent attached a clip. Shows a guy going through the desk who looks like you.'

'Like me?' said Jacob. 'Wow, that's funny.'

'You don't quite see him take the knife, but – how should I put it – the dots are there to be connected.'

'Okay,' said Jacob.

'I'm not saying it's you. If I knew it was you, I'd have to report it, right?'

'It wasn't me.'

'Shut up,' said Tom. 'Can't you tell when someone's doing you a favour? I'm calling to give you advice. Stop looking at houses. Like, immediately.'

Jacob started thinking of next steps. 'If they got the knife back, you think they might let it go?'

'That's not my problem,' said Tom. 'Listen, say goodbye to your wife for me. She seemed nice.' He hung up without another word.

Jacob went to the nearest window and stared out, trying to gather himself. Rain streaked the glass, and the fluorescent lights above him buzzed, giving the library a fish-tank vibe. He needed to ditch the knife.

When he reached their street, the rain had turned torrential and the closest parking spot was half a block from the townhouse. He sprinted to the front door and fumbled with his keys, only to discover it wasn't locked. Inside, Meleka's shoes were gone from the mat, replaced by a pair of wet sneakers he didn't recognize.

Then he heard the couch springs groan.

The curtains in the living room had been drawn, as they always were during sessions, but Meleka wasn't there. From the couch, the kid looked at him with owlish eyes. He sat straight-backed, shirt and jeans soaked through, hair limply framing his face.

'Where's Meleka?' Jacob asked.

The kid shrugged.

Jacob knew he'd catch hell if he started a conversation, so he left and searched the house. No sign of her downstairs or in the backyard. The thought that the kid had been in their home unsupervised made him queasy. He went upstairs and checked the bedrooms, the bathroom, the linen closet. The knife still lay under the towels. He put it in his pocket and returned to the living room.

'Were you having a session?' he asked.

'We were supposed to,' the kid said. 'I couldn't get hold of her.'

That brought Jacob up short. 'Didn't she let you in?'

The kid shook his head. 'The door was open.'

Jacob couldn't believe it. 'So you just walked in here?'

The kid didn't blink. 'It was raining. This is where we meet.'

'Did she know you were coming?'

The kid drew a breath, like he was losing patience with a wilful child. 'I texted, but she didn't answer.'

'Stay there,' Jacob said. 'I'm going to call her.'

When he phoned from the kitchen, the call went right to voicemail.

'The kid's in our living room,' he said. 'I think he might have broken in. Where are you?' Then he texted her: *The kid has invaded our house.* He stood and waited. No response.

In the living room, the kid was seated as before, staring at Meleka's empty chair. It was only then that Jacob spotted her keys on the coffee table.

'Were those there the whole time?' he asked. She always insisted on locking up when they went out, even if only to the corner store.

The kid looked at the keys awhile. 'Yeah,' he said.

'You didn't use them to get in?'

The kid's face stayed blank. 'How could I when they were there the whole time?'

Jacob wanted to tell him not to be a smartass. He hated having to pussyfoot. His hand slid into his pocket. The smooth polish of the knife handle gave him a sudden sense of freedom.

'So you've been groping women,' he said.

As soon as he spoke the words, he knew he shouldn't have.

'She told you that?' the kid said.

Jacob considered nodding, but he decided to play it safe. 'It's what people are saying.'

'Really? Are they also saying you were her patient?'

Jacob felt his blood rise. 'What are you talking about?'

'Bro, she told me she was your therapist.'

A lump swelled in Jacob's throat. His fingers squeezed the knife.

Behind him, the front door opened. Meleka stepped inside, dragging her favourite suitcase over the threshold. It must have stopped raining, because she didn't look wet. She seemed to register the kid's sneakers before anything else, just as Jacob had done. Then she pivoted toward the living room.

'Devin,' she said. 'What's going on?'

The kid rose from the couch. 'I called you, but you didn't answer.'

'My mobile was switched off.'

'I called, too,' said Jacob. 'He was sitting here when I got home.'

She turned to peer out through the open door. 'Both of you wait here,' she said. 'I have to pay the taxi driver.' Then she left again, abandoning her suitcase on the mat.

If Jacob had been alone, he'd have snuck a glance out through the curtains. Instead, he and the kid stood in place. There was the tick-tock of footsteps returning before they retreated again, followed by the thud of a trunk closing and a car driving away. A few seconds later, she re-entered the house.

'I need to talk with Devin,' she said.

'Sure,' said Jacob. 'I'll be in the kitchen.'

He went there but lingered only a few seconds before moving to the dining room to put his ear against the wall. The kid was saying something he couldn't make out. The couch wheezed, and then all noise dropped away.

After a minute, it occurred to him that the kid and Meleka had left the house. The whole time, they'd been planning to take off together. Maybe a mix-up over where to meet had brought her back. Jacob had blown his chance to stop them. Where would they go? Australia, probably. He'd get the divorce papers in the mail.

Turning, he caught the edge of one of the stacked boxes with his elbow. As it hit the floor, he heard something inside break. Glass? Pottery? He hadn't bothered to label the boxes, and he couldn't remember what they held. He thought of taking out the knife to slice open the cardboard and see what he'd destroyed. There were too many boxes in this room. He'd have to get rid of them soon; he wouldn't be able to handle living with them on his own.

A moment later, Meleka's voice came through the wall. He pressed close to listen.

'Last night, my parents asked me what I was doing here,' she said. 'They don't slag you off anymore, they just ask questions. I told them how nice it was, finally having somebody who puts me first. I don't think they even noticed the insinuation. My being here frightens them. I was always such a well-behaved child. I never took risks. I never felt I was allowed them. Now, I don't know what's going on.'

The armchair creaked beneath her. 'I'm sorry, Jacob,' she said. 'I appreciate that you can't help yourself – even what you're doing now.'

He hurried from the dining room. She was already at the front door, putting on her shoes. He glanced into the living room. The kid was gone, and his sneakers had vanished from the mat.

Jacob didn't know what to say. When she opened the door, he saw the rest of her suitcases sitting on the step. She picked up the biggest one and heaved it inside.

'For what it's worth, my phone really was off,' she said. 'I didn't come back because of Devin. I changed my mind.'

Jacob weighed her words. Then he stepped through the door-way and reached for her. 'Thank you for coming back,' he said.

After a while, they brought in the rest of the cases.

'You got here just in time,' he said, trying to make a joke of it. 'Any minute, the kid was going to grope me.'

'I saved the day,' she said.

'You did,' he agreed. 'You saved me.'

As he made dinner, he could hear her upstairs, unpacking. When she came down to eat, she barely touched her food.

'Hey – knock, knock,' he said.

She shook her head and began to laugh. It was too much laughter, like he wasn't there.

'Come on, wait for the punchline,' he said. 'Knock, knock.'

'Sorry,' she replied, turning sober. 'Who's there?'

'Fix your doorbell,' he said. 'I've been ringing it for half an hour.'

But she'd ruined the timing, and they fell back into silence. Once he'd finished eating, rather than starting into the clean-up, he said that he had to run an errand across town, and she nodded without asking any questions.

It was dark by the time he parked outside the place on Cranbrook. The sellers were home; they hadn't yet drawn the blinds, so he could see them moving through the rooms: a middle-aged couple and two teenage boys. He worried that one of them might open the front door just as he reached the mailbox next to it, but he got out of the car anyway, carrying a manila envelope with the knife inside. He doubted that the family would take things further if they had it back. Still, he wore gloves, and he'd wiped down the handle. Wasn't the nanny cam a sign of someone treating things far too seriously? Proof that everybody was nuts in one way or another, the everyday sanity balanced out by little bailiwicks of craziness.

Driving home, he took the longer route. He didn't think about why until he saw the kid's street ahead. Jacob knew the address from Meleka's files. The kid lived on the fifth floor of a condo building. The two other nights Jacob had come by, the lights had been on.

This time, when he parked and looked up at the apartment, the windows were dark. It was a little disappointing. Jacob wanted the reassurance of seeing the kid where he was supposed to be. He wanted to be soothed by the habits and rhythms of someone else's life. Then again, it might turn out for the best that the evening granted him no reason to linger. The thought of Meleka alone with all those suitcases was making him jumpy, and he needed to get home.

ACKNOWLEDGEMENTS

The sentence fragment that Cam reads and misreads in 'The Isle of Thanet' is my translation of a line from Rainer Maria Rilke's *Letters to a Young Poet*.

Many thanks to Alana Wilcox and the crew at Coach House Books for their care and expertise in bringing this collection into the world. Thanks also to Euan Thorneycroft and the team at A. M. Heath for all their work on my behalf.

I'm grateful to the magazines that first published versions of stories appearing here: *The Atlantic, Descant, The Dublin Review, The Fiddlehead, Grain, Hazlitt, The New Quarterly, Prairie Fire,* and PRISM *International*.

For wisdom, support, and encouragement at key moments, I owe debts to André Alexis, Katherine Ashenburg, Clive Card, Lindsay Eaglesham, Brenda Foster, J. M. Gamble, Keith Gilbert, Ron Graham, Frances Greenslade, Elizabeth Hay, Michael Helm, Linton Kwesi Johnson, John Kelly, Kathryn Kuitenbrouwer, George Logan, Alexander MacLeod, Andrew Motion, Noor Naga, Andrew Pyper, Michael Redhill, Tanis Rideout, Laura Robinson, Alexandra Rockingham, Gary Ross, W. G. Sebald, Ulrica Skagert, Carolyn Smart, Ali Smith, Zadie Smith, David Staines, John Thieme, Aritha van Herk, Joy Ward, Tracy Ware, Ian Williams, and Michael Winter. Thanks to my fellow writers in Oxford and East Anglia for long-ago workshop feedback and to my colleagues and students at the University of Toronto for daily inspiration. I'm grateful to the Bergman Estate on Fårö for giving me time and space in which to write, the Social Sciences and Humanities Research Council of Canada for Insight Grant funding, and the Jackman Humanities Institute for a fellowship that made finishing this book possible.

Thanks to Michael Bianchi, Nicholas Bradley, Shawn Brady, Derek Caveney, Geordie Farrell, Paul Felix, Ronald Fitzpatrick,

John Fraser, Megan Frederickson, Audrey Giles, Marco Gualtieri, Todd Jackson, Robert Juričević, Julia Markovits, Moen Mohamed, Dragana Obradović, Grace O'Connell, Reecia Orzeck, and Blake Williams for their constancy. Thanks, too, to my family and Fiona Coll.

Robert McGill is the author of the novels *The Mysteries, Once We Had a Country*, and *A Suitable Companion for the End of Your Life*, as well as of two nonfiction books, *The Treacherous Imagination* and *War Is Here*. His stories 'Confidence Men' and 'The Stars Are Falling' were chosen for *The Journey Prize Anthology*, and 'Nobody Goes to Vancouver to Die' was shortlisted for a National Magazine Award. He teaches at the University of Toronto. Visit him at robert-mcgill.com.

Typeset in Whitman and Atrament.

Printed at the Coach House on bpNichol Lane in Toronto, Ontario, on Zephyr Antique Laid paper, which was manufactured, acid-free, in Saint-Jérôme, Quebec, from second-growth forests. This book was printed with vegetable-based ink on a 1973 Heidelberg KORD offset litho press. Its pages were folded on a Baumfolder, gathered by hand, bound on a Sulby Auto-Minabinda, and trimmed on a Polar single-knife cutter.

Coach House is located in Toronto, which is on the traditional territory of many nations, including the Mississaugas of the Credit, the Anishnabeg, the Chippewa, the Haudenosaunee, and the Wendat peoples, and is now home to many diverse First Nations, Inuit, and Métis peoples. We acknowledge that Toronto is covered by Treaty 13 with the Mississaugas of the Credit. We are grateful to live and work on this land.

Edited by Alana Wilcox
Cover design by Natalie Olsen, Kisscut Design
Interior design by Crystal Sikma
Author photo by Fiona Coll

Coach House Books
80 bpNichol Lane
Toronto ON M5S 3J4
Canada

mail@chbooks.com
www.chbooks.com